An Unexpected Kind

An Unexpected Kind

by

Angela K Parker

This is a work of fiction. Names, characters, businesses, places, events, and incidents are either the products of the author's imagination or used in a fictitious manner. Any resemblance to actual persons, living or dead, or actual events is purely coincidental.

Published: Angela K. Parker 2018
angelaparkerauthor@gmail.com

"Cover Design ©Dark Water Covers"
ISBN: 978-1719500968

Dedication

To finding love after heartbreak.

Preface

This is a story about friendship, love, acceptance, and heartbreak. The main characters, Bradley and Samantha's journey, both begin at a turning point in their lives. While Bradley comes to accept love, Samantha wants nothing to do with it.

In part one, they take us back two years, to their previous relationships with Valerie and Garrett. We get to experience how it all started and witness the events that shaped who they are now.

In part two, Bradley and Samantha meet for the first time. It's new territory for both of them, and they have to decipher what these new feelings mean.

Table of Contents

Chapter 1	1
Chapter 2	8
Chapter 3	12
Chapter 4	15
Chapter 5	21
Chapter 6	24
Chapter 7	26
Chapter 8	31
Chapter 9	37
Chapter 10	43
Chapter 11	49
Chapter 12	55
Chapter 13	62
Chapter 14	69
Chapter 15	75
Chapter 16	81
Chapter 17	88
Chapter 18	94
Chapter 19	99
Chapter 20	108

Chapter 21	119
Chapter 22	127
Part Two	135
Chapter 23	136
Chapter 24	146
Chapter 25	151
Chapter 26	158
Chapter 27	164
Chapter 28	172
Chapter 29	179
Chapter 30	189
Chapter 31	196
Chapter 32	203
Until Next Time...	212
About the Author	213
Connect with the Author	214

Part One

Friendship & Betrayal

Bradley & Valerie

Samantha & Garrett

Chapter 1

Bradley

Present Day

I had a plan for my life, a well thought out plan that didn't include love until I reached the age of twenty-nine. According to my timeline, after I finished high school, it would take me eight years to get through undergrad and grad school. I would use the last year to get established and prepare for whatever comes after.

All of my life, I've wanted to be a mathematician. Something about numbers had always excited me. Most of my peers are surprised to learn that about me, but they respect me for who I am.

I had plenty of friends, went to parties, and did normal things kids my age did. I had also spent a great amount of time with my face shoved between the pages of books. I didn't have a bad life, but I had watched my parents struggle to get where they are. I wanted to do better, be better, and they wanted that for me too.

My parents, Clifford and Laura, are not the perfect couple. I had witnessed countless arguments and disagreements over the years. One memory stands out like a sore thumb, a memory that changed my way of thinking and influenced the course of my life. I was young, but I still remember it like it was yesterday.

I was fourteen at that time. My mom was a cashier at a local grocery store. At the time, mom's car was in the shop for repairs. Dad was the driver for all of us. Dad and I had gone to pick her up from work that evening. When we got there, mom was standing outside, talking to some man. The man's hand was gently placed on her shoulder, and he looked at her with such admiration. Her smile was bright, and she looked genuinely happy.

At home, mom was always busy. She rarely took a moment for herself, and her smiles weren't plenty. That day when we picked her up from work, my heart was full. It had been a while since I'd seen that smile. It wasn't until years later when I saw that smile again.

When we got home that evening, mom and dad barely spoke. I could sense that something was off. My dad was a casual drinker, but that night at dinner, he drank too much.

Mom had put us, kids, to bed, but I was curious. I couldn't sleep, especially when I heard the raised voices. I don't know what they were arguing about, but I recognized the words spoken that shouldn't have been said.

I heard the front door slam shut when my dad stormed out.

I witnessed the tears that my mom shed as I exited my room to comfort her.

My dad was not a drunk, but that night he drank too much.

He left that night and stayed away for weeks. My mom was a wreck, and I didn't understand how my dad could hurt her like that. My child mind hated him for it. I wasn't supposed to be the one to make her happy, but I tried. I shouldn't have had to pick up his slack because he left, but I did.

When he came back weeks later, they acted as if none of it ever happened. That simple act made me pull away from my dad, as well as my mom. I was angry with him for leaving and thinking he could just come back without an explanation. I couldn't understand how she could let him back in after all of the pain he had caused. How could she forgive so easily?

I vowed that day to never be like my parents.

Drinking caused pain. Alcohol would never touch my lips.

Love hurts and makes you do stupid things. My heart would never fully belong to another person.

My parents were weak, and I wouldn't make the same mistake. When I was ready to love, it would be on my terms, and half of my heart would always belong to me because surrendering to love is a weakness.

That wasn't the last argument they had, but it was the only time he left. That was the only time I ever saw my dad drunk. My mom quit her job when my dad came back, and it was years later before her smile met her eyes again.

My sisters, Ginger and Haley, stayed asleep that night. They didn't witness the harsh scene. They never heard my mom's cry. When they woke up, dad was gone, and I had to pick up the pieces. My impression of him was tarnished, but I didn't want my sisters to feel the same way. They adored our dad, and for some reason, I couldn't take that away from them. My mom was in no condition to explain, so I lied. I told them that dad was on a business trip, and he didn't say how long he would be gone. Mom was sick, and they needed to keep their distance. I had to take care of her while dad was away.

Three years have passed since that night. We have all moved on, but I have never forgotten.

"BP!" Gin shouts like I'm not standing inches away from her. "Would you mind dropping me off at Jeremy's on your way to school? He's taking me out tonight."

I slide my sister, Ginger, an amused glance at the nickname she gave me. She's been calling me that since she was old enough to know better. It used to annoy me when I was younger, but I have grown to like it over the years. I can still recall her saying, *"BP, just like the gas station."* In turn, I began calling her Gin, just like the label on our dad's spirit bottle.

Gin and I grew up like twins. We always joke with my parents about how close we are in age. My mom had me, and ten months later, Gin came along. We've had our share of arguments and fights growing up, but we were always thick as thieves. She kept my secrets, and I kept hers. I could always count on her even when I had no one else. We're still that way today. We've chosen different paths in life, but she will always be my closest friend.

"Actually, I do mind, Gin."

"But you're going to do it anyway because I'm your best friend."

"The jury is still out on that, but yes, I will take you. I don't think I have a choice. Mom has an event, and dad has to be in the office early this morning."

A few months after mom quit her job as a cashier, she took up event planning as a hobby, and it flourished into a career. Dad is an electrician. His hours fluctuate quite a bit.

"Great! I knew I could count on you," she says playfully.

"Where are you guys going anyway?"

"I don't know. It's our anniversary. He wants it to be a surprise."

Gin and Jeremy are the picture-perfect couple. She has always been a romantic at heart, unlike me. She believes in happily ever after. She believes in soulmates and instant connections.

I'm not sure if Jeremy believes in that stuff, but he makes her happy. He keeps her safe. He has never hurt her, and that's all that matters. As long as he stays on that course, I don't have a problem with him.

"Do me a favor, will you, Gin?"

"I already know what you're going to say, BP," Gin drags out.

"You do, huh?" I give her a sideways glance.

"The same thing you say every time I go out with Jeremy. Don't bring you back any surprises," Gin says mockingly.

"So, you do listen when I talk. I was beginning to wonder."

"Don't worry your pretty little head about me. Jeremy and I are…" She pauses and wiggles her brows. "Safe."

"What are you two talking about?"

Our younger sister, Haley, enters, and I jerk my head in her direction. Haley is three years younger than us. She is the most innocent and reserved out of the three of us. That's what I like most about her. My plan is to keep her that way. Gin, on the other hand, does everything she can to try and corrupt her.

Gin grabs a banana from the fruit bowl and waves it through the air.

"Do you really want to know Hale?"

"Gin," I say in warning.

Gin looks at me and giggles.

"Don't worry, prude. I wasn't going to say anything improper. You know, you should really loosen up. She has to learn someday." She glances over to Haley. "Don't be naïve, BP. She may act innocent, but trust me. She knows more than you think."

She peels the banana, takes a bite, and walks away.

I yell after her. "I'm leaving in ten minutes, Gin."

"I didn't mean to disrupt your conversation," Hale says.

"You didn't. Gin was just being her usual self. It wasn't important."

"Where is she going?"

"She and Jeremy are going out after school. Do you want to ride with us this morning?"

"No, I'll take the bus. My best ideas are formed on the bus," Hale says with a cheeky grin.

Haley is a dreamer. She believes all things are possible. She's focused, driven and she doesn't let anything stand in her way when she wants something. I don't like to boast, but I would like to think that she gets the latter from me. We don't talk as much as Gin and me, probably because of the age difference. I don't really know what to say to her, other than the normal greeting.

There are a few seconds of awkward silence hanging in the air between us. "If you change your mind, I'm leaving in less than ten minutes."

Hale grabs an apple and walks out the door, ignoring my last statement.

Some teenage girls are so hard to figure out, I think to myself. I've only had one relationship, and it did nothing to help me decipher girls. If anything, I'm more confused now than ever. They are all unique… always wanting something different and something more.

Chapter 2

Samantha

Present Day

I never had a chance to know my mother. She died giving birth to me. My father raised me and my sister, Lacy, alone. I often wonder how I can miss something I never had, but I do. I've seen pictures and heard stories, but it did little to ease the hole in my heart.

No one has ever said the words to me, but I have always felt like it is my fault that she's not here.

I grew up wanting to be just like her. I took my family's memories of her and made them a part of me. She was an athlete, and I wanted to be one too. That's why I joined the swim team and worked my way up to team captain. Even though she's not here, I want her and my family to be proud of me. It's the least that I can do for causing her death. I'm determined that her death will not be in vain.

In my eyes, my father is the strongest man I know. He could've made excuses when my mother died, but he didn't. He stuck around and remained present in every aspect of our lives. There was never a moment when I didn't feel loved. There was never anything I needed that I didn't have.

My sister, Lacy, is eight years older than me. She has been a big help to both my dad and me. Instead of her going away to college, she decided to attend a local college after graduation. She has always been there to step in when my father had to work, along with my grandparents.

Lacy is my inspiration. Though I can't help but feel guilty when I look at her. She's one more person that gave up their life for me. She's the best sister a girl can have, and she's also a great role model. I'll never know my mother, but I feel like God gave me the next best thing with Lacy.

We've never talked about why she took on the role she did. I'll be forever grateful. It couldn't have been easy for an eight-year-old, who had just lost her mother, to accept the baby that took her away.

Lacy moved out of the house after she received her degree and later got married. She works at a bank in town as an account manager. She still stops in daily to check on dad and me. I sometimes wonder if that will ever change.

I smile when I hear the front door open. This is one of the highlights of my day.

"Dad, is that you?" I call out to him just as I do every day. I know it's him, but it's become our daily routine.

"How is my Sammy doing today?" His response is always the same.

I love these moments, his cheery smile and gentle bear hugs.

"Sammy had a great day, dad." My smile is just as bright.

"What's on the agenda for tonight?"

Every day is special with my dad, but Fridays have become a thing for the three of us. With the possibility of college lurking near, I know days like this will be few and far between. It's a dreaded happiness. On the one hand, I'm excited about school, and my dad can finally have his life back. On the other hand, I will miss him, and his life won't be full of Sammy anymore. I worry about what he will do when I'm gone.

"Lacy should be here any minute now. There is no need to break tradition just yet; dinner and a movie, it shall be."

"Great. I'm going to freshen up and get comfortable. Don't start without me."

"I wouldn't dare to think it. It wouldn't be the same without you."

When Lacy arrives, she looks me over and gives me a motherly hug. She made it a habit years ago to assess me when she hasn't seen me all day. I imagine it's what our mother would've been like.

"How was your day, Grace?"

Lacy is the only one who calls me by my middle name. I always thought it was because it resembled hers. Maybe it makes her feel closer to me in some way. She looks just like our mother. I was blessed with most of my father's features. I guess it's fitting since I'm a daddy's girl. I don't have the same motherly instincts as Lacy does. That's the only thing I didn't want to inherit from my mother. I believe that love exists and would like to be married one day, but I don't think that I will ever have children. I'm afraid of history repeating itself.

"It was good, as usual. What about you? Anything interesting?"

"No, not at all, which is probably a good thing, considering where I work."

"Well, dad will be down in a minute. I'm glad you could make it."

"I wouldn't miss it for anything in the world, especially now with you getting older. These days are precious."

Lacy gives me a sad smile and breathes deeply. I know what she's thinking because I've been thinking about it a lot lately as well.

When dad joins us, we settle in the living room for an evening of fun with our chicken wings and fries.

These are the days I will miss the most.

Chapter 3

Bradley

Two Years Earlier

Mr. Carr's class is one of my least favorite classes. It wasn't the subject matter that annoyed me. It was the way he taught the subject. He made fifty minutes of history feel like hours.

I guess I have Mr. Carr to thank for my latest distraction. Before History, I would go into every class with one purpose; to focus and learn all that I could to keep my A average. There is no such thing as focus in Mr. Carr's class, at least not for me. It was so bad that I began people watching in class. I was curious to know if it was just me. I found out I was not alone.

History class is where I discovered Valerie. I had never noticed her before. I had never really noticed anyone before; until the day I got so bored that I had no other choice. She sat at a slight angle on the left side of the room across from me. The twirl of her pencil through her fingertips caught my eyes. A quick look at her face told me she was just as interested in history as I was. She was staring off into space, which brought a chuckle out of me.

I'll never forget the irate look that Mr. Carr shot at me that day. I had never been in trouble before. So, for him to give his prize student the look, well, let's just say the entire class was in a fit of laughter. All except Valerie. She smiled at me, but her gaze showed curiosity. I wondered if she had ever noticed me before. I was curious as to what she was thinking and what that look meant.

After two weeks of wondering, my curiosity got the best of me. I waited in the hall after class for her to exit.

"Valerie."

I spoke her name for the first time, and she turned to look at me. I had never been that close to her before.

"You're Bradley, right?"

Hearing her say my name didn't spark any fires, but I could sense there was something in her. I needed her in my life. I didn't know how, but I did.

"Yeah."

"What can I do for you, Bradley?"

"I was wondering if you would like to hang out with me sometimes."

She gave me that curious look that I remember from the first day. Her eyes squinted, and lips twisted to one side.

"Why would you want to hang out with me, Bradley? You've never said one word to me before. What makes today special?"

This was the first time that Valerie got a rise out of me. It wasn't anything sexual. I admired the way she took charge of the conversation. Looking at her from across the room, I wouldn't have known how sharp her bite was. She was always so quiet, and all I could manage to get out of her was a smile. If there were a female version of me, she would be it. That drew me to her even more.

"Maybe I was tired of the way you constantly stared my way in class. Misery can be a torturous thing. I thought it would be best if I squashed it before it became too unbearable for you."

She belts out a laugh, and I join in.

"Very smooth Bradley, very smooth. Do you talk to all of the girls this way?"

"To be truthful, no. Now, what do you say? Will you be my hang woman?"

That makes her laugh even harder. Valerie's laughter draws the attention of everyone close by.

"That was such a cheesy line Bradley. We'll have to work on that."

"Does that mean, yes?"

"It depends, are we hanging out or *hanging out*?"

"Hanging out. We can be study partners, friends, or best friends. I just feel like you need me in some way."

"Hah, *I* need you? The only reason we're having this conversation is because you approached me, remember?"

"That's only because you wouldn't stop staring."

"Sure Bradley, we can hang out but let's get one thing straight, I don't need you."

"Sure, you don't."

I can clearly see that this is the beginning of a beautiful friendship. Valerie is right. She doesn't need me. At this stage in my life, I need her. She will be my best distraction.

Chapter 4

Samantha

Present Day

I was fourteen when I first laid eyes on Garrett Wright. He was leaning against the lockers, surrounded by a group of girls. He was the type of guy that showed up in every girl's dreams. I was the type of girl that he would never think twice about. That thought didn't stop me from fantasizing. I didn't know the first thing about him, but I was obviously drawn in by his good looks and charm.

We were both new to this high school, but I later found out why Garrett was so well known. Garrett's older brother Terrance James, or TJ as everyone called him, was the star quarterback. He was a looker as well, but he didn't have the same charm as Garrett. Garrett had the kind of charm that could make you melt with just one look. Though he was known as TJ's little brother, he quickly made his name known. He even managed to catch the eyes of some of the older girls.

I attended nearly every football game, just so I could watch Garrett run up and down the field. I didn't know much about the sport at first, but I've learned plenty since meeting him. I longed to be his all throughout ninth grade. He never acknowledged me until he needed my help. Like his brother, Garrett joined the football team, but he had trouble keeping up with his grades.

Tenth grade was the year I met Garrett Wright. By this time, he had sprouted muscles everywhere, and his facial hair had grown in. His short blonde locks were icing on the cake. He was gorgeous. The moment I agreed to help him with his math, I knew I was in trouble.

Garrett didn't have a girlfriend, but he had plenty of suitors. Looking back now, I don't know what I was thinking. If I had put any thought into it, I would have realized that he could never be who I expected him to be. He could never be a kept guy, but I tried my best to make it happen. Every moment I spent with him is etched into my memory; the good and the bad.

***

Two Years Earlier

I couldn't wait to get to math class every day. It was one of two classes that I had with Garrett. It's been a year, and he still hasn't noticed me. Who could blame him? It's not like I'm throwing myself at him, as all of the other girls do. I could probably play dress up and beg for his attention, but that's not who I am. I want him to notice me without all of the efforts.

Here he is now, escorted by Cindy & Michelle, the cheer captain, and her sidekick. He has an arm draped around each of their shoulders. I wonder what it would feel like to have those arms wrapped around me. They walk past me to the rear of the class without one glance my way. I don't know what he sees in them. What do they have that I don't?

This is the hard part, hearing the giggles behind me and being unable to see what's going on. I can only imagine as Mrs. Miller shoots a stern look towards the back of the class. The laughing ceases when she clears her throat.

"Mr. Wright, is there something that you'd like to share with the rest of the class?"

Mrs. Miller is my favorite teacher. She's a take-charge kind of lady and her students respect her. There is never trouble in her classroom, and all it takes is a few words to stop anyone from getting out of order.

"No, ma'am," comes Garrett's response.

His voice gives me butterflies. I want so badly to turn around and see his expression.

"Great. Now let us begin."

Mrs. Miller begins her lesson, and I think one final thought before I switch my focus. *Oh, what I wouldn't give to be at the back of the class right now.*

I'm usually one of the first ones to walk out of the door, but Mrs. Miller asks me to stay behind when the bell rings today.

"Samantha, can I see you for a few minutes?"

I follow her eyes back to Garrett, who's whispering something into Michelle's ear.

"Garrett, I need a few minutes of your time."

My heartbeat picks up. I'm all types of confused and excited, wondering what this could be about. Why does she need to see us… together?

I stay seated when everyone else leaves. It's lunch break. So, we won't be disturbed by a rush of students entering the class. Garrett takes the seat right next to me, and my body stiffens. I've never been this close to him before. I focus my attention on Mrs. Miller as she begins to speak.

"Garrett, coach Johnson has informed me that you need some additional help with this class, or you'll be kicked off of the football team. While you're not failing, a D is not acceptable for those participating in our athletics program."

She gives me a friendly smile.

"Which is why you are here, Samantha. You are one of my brightest and most attentive students, and you seem to pick up things quickly. Would you be interested in joining our tutoring program?"

I'm still stuck on the fact that Garrett is sitting next to me. "What would that entail exactly?"

"It's not mandatory. You would be listed as one of the school's tutors. When the students seek out our help, you will be presented with the option to either accept or decline the assignment. It is required that you commit at least eight hours to the program per school term, to be eligible for the scholarship and miscellaneous rewards."

I perk up at the mention of a scholarship. My first thought goes to my dad. He's done so much for me already. This scholarship could really help out, regardless of the amount.

"There's a scholarship?"

"Yes. We can discuss that in detail if you decide it's something you want to do."

"I'm interested."

"That's great because Garrett could use your help. Do the two of you know each other?"

I know *all* about Garrett Wright, but I wouldn't dare shout it from the mountaintops. Garrett surprises me with his response.

"No, but we have two classes together."

Heat.

Heat.

Heat.

It's so hot in here.

Garrett Wright noticed me.

I open my mouth to speak, but nothing comes out.

"Samantha, if you do decide to help Garrett, this will count toward your required hours. So, what do you say? Are you ready to take on your first student, or do you need some more time to think about it?"

Do I need to think about it?

"No, I'll do it."

Isn't this what I've been wanting... to get close to Garrett? This is my chance and probably the only one I'll ever get.

"Garrett, are you okay with Samantha as your tutor?"

I chance a look at Garrett and am greeted with a smile I can't help but return. He looks me over from head to toe, and the butterflies go haywire inside of me, but I remain calm. I can't believe this is happening.

"I'm good with it if she is. I think we could both learn from this… experience."

Garrett and I are engaged in a staring contest when we are pulled away by a loud clap.

"I have some paperwork for you both to fill out. Then we can set up times and dates for the two of you to meet. The other students usually meet during lunch break or after school. If you have free time on the weekends, that's also acceptable."

The idea of me spending any time with Garrett is a dream come true.

Chapter 5

Bradley

Two Years Earlier

Val and I have been hanging out after school most days for the past month. She's as close to me as I will allow her to get. She doesn't seem to mind. We are both on the same page when it comes to relationships. Neither of us wants to be tied down, but it's nice to have someone else to talk to. Since Gin met Jeremy, we don't spend as much time together. Valerie has become my listening ear and me hers.

Val rolls a strike and turns to face me.

"In your face," she shouts. "See if you can top that."

I'm competitive when it comes to bowling, and she knows it. She's the only one who's ever beat me. My game is always off when I'm around Val. My friendly frustration is boiling over.

"Oh, I can, and I will."

She grins behind me as I slip my fingers through the holes in the ball and step up to the lane. I have to get a strike to win the game.

I pull my arm back and let the ball roll straight down the center lane, hitting the center pin. Nine pins fall, and I hold my breath as the final pin wobbles and straightens back into its' normal position.

"I win! I win!" Val sings behind me.

I'm not able to back up my words, but I feel an inkling of joy seeing Val so happy. She keeps me smiling, even when I don't have much to smile about.

"That's only because my arm is hurting," I lie.

"Uhm, sure it is. Tell that to someone who will believe it."

"It's true. You pack a mean punch."

"Are you kidding me right now? That was hours ago. Are you saying that you can't take a punch from a girl?"

Val folds her arms across her chest and raises a brow. She's so cute when she's like this.

"Those were not my words Val. I can take a punch from any girl, but you, my friend, hit like a guy. I think you need to give the boxing class a rest."

Her whole demeanor changes with my statement. Val picks and chooses what she tells me, and I respect that. I've asked her before why she chose boxing. She did share with me that she's had a difficult past. Her mother suggested boxing classes as a way of letting off steam, and she would learn how to protect herself in the process.

Val is not an ordinary teenage girl. I could sense that about her from the moment I met her. She is as tough as nails and as strong as steel. She has a wall around her heart, just as I do. Our friendship isn't fully developed yet, but I'm hoping it will be one day. I want her to be able to trust me with her secrets. When she is ready to let me in, I will be there for her.

I swing my arm around her neck and pull her into my side.

"Come on, She-Ra. Let's go eat."

She relaxes beside me. I don't know what happened in her past to cause that type of reaction, but I'm glad I'm able to ease her tension.

Chapter 6

Samantha

Two Years Earlier

I can do this. I can do this. There is no need to be nervous. Garrett is just a guy. I repeat the mantra over and over in my head, praying it will help calm the butterflies within me.

Saying yes and filling out the paperwork was the easy part. The knowledge of having one on one sessions with Garrett is quite the opposite. I've been on autopilot from the moment I found out that he knew who I was two days ago.

The library is fairly empty after school. A few students are wandering around, catching up on late or missed assignments.

Garrett and I decided to meet here in the evenings to make it easier for him to get to football practice on time. I go to my usual quiet spot off to the side, near the windows. The empty field outside is not much of a view right now, but I need something else to focus on if I get distracted by Garrett.

I freeze when a shadow falls over me. The voice inside my head telling me no is not strong enough to steer me away from Garrett. I turn to face him when he sits across from me. Blonde hair *and* blue eyes… I'm definitely in trouble.

I know my feelings for him are dangerous, but I have to see this through. I can control my raging hormones. I'm not foolish enough to think that Garrett would fall for someone like me.

"Hello, Samantha."

I swallow deeply when my name leaves his mouth.

"Hi, Garrett," I manage to respond. I glance at his lips and quickly look up to his beautiful eyes.

"So, where do we start?" he asks.

"That depends on your weakness. What areas do you need help with?"

Garrett sports a cocky smirk like I've never seen before. I can't tell what he's thinking, but I know exactly what that smirk does to my thoughts.

"I could use your help with many things, Samantha, and I don't particularly like being tested, but for you, I think I can endure it."

I've watched Garrett in action with the other girls around school, but I now realize that he is even more of a flirt up close. I pretend that I'm not affected by his comment.

"I made a practice test just in case. Do you want to start with that? The results from that should give me an idea of where you are and what you need help with."

I sit up straighter in my chair. I can do this. I'm about to give Garrett a test, and while I'm testing him, he has no idea about the test he's putting me through. I'm not a quitter, and this is one test I plan to pass with flying colors.

Chapter 7

Bradley

Two Years Earlier

Since my mom made a career out of planning events, she doesn't let our birthdays pass without making a big deal out of it. A little birdie named Hale told me days ago that mom has a surprise party scheduled for me after school. She only invited a few family members. Hale knows that I don't like surprises. Anything she knows that will affect me, she always spills the beans before the occasion.

I have taken the liberty of inviting Val over. I left out the part about the party on purpose. She hates surprises as well. She's been over to my house before, but this will be the first time she's greeted by a mob of family members. Her reaction will be my gift to me. I know her expression will be priceless, and I'm sure she will make me pay for it, but it's totally going to be worth it.

Val and I go to the local library for our study session before going to my house. Before I met her, I studied on my own, usually at home, enclosed in my room. That's where our study sessions began but in the family room instead of my bedroom.

My mom scoffed at the idea of me having a girl in my room alone. She says she's not ready to be a grandma just yet. I think it's funny. Val and I are nowhere near that level of commitment.

We couldn't get much studying done with doors continuously being opened and closed. There was also an issue with prying eyes; the constant need to know what we were doing and when we would be done.

I love my family, but sometimes I just need a break. I was forced to grow up far too fast. With Val, I feel like I'm able to breathe and live out my childhood like normal kids my age.

The only cars in the driveway when we pull up are those of my parents and Jeremy.

I wonder where they housed all of the cars. I go over my reaction in my mind right before I open the door. The voices scream out, *"surprise!"* and Val is stock-still beside me. Her expression… the best birthday gift ever. I widen my eyes and take a step back, giving my best impression of shock.

Val squeaks quietly in front of me. "Oh, my God!"

That's as quiet as I've ever heard Val speak. She's not one to hold back.

We step inside, and I close the door behind us. My mom is front and center with a huge smile on her face. She leads the birthday song, and everyone else follows.

I glance quickly around the room. Gin, Hale, and mom's parents are standing right next to her. I knew my dad's parents wouldn't be here. They live too far away for a day trip in the middle of the week. My aunts, Lisa and Lindsey, are here, along with my uncles, Fred and Bill.

Hale's best friend, Amy, is here. She has a huge crush on me, but I pretend I don't notice. I think it's kind of cute, the way she watches me.

My eyes continue to scan the room. I see some of my cousins jumping up and down. My dad is posted up in the rear of the room. He's not a singer, but he looks on proudly as everyone else finishes off the song. I'm surprised to see a smile on his face, especially directed at me. My dad and I haven't been close for years. I still blame him for what happened. He has tried to connect with me, but I can't bring myself to forgive him for walking out on mom.

"Happy birthday, son," mom says as she throws her arms around me. "I can't believe you're all grown up."

"I'm only sixteen, mom."

"I know, but soon you will be a man, and you'll be moving away to start your adult life."

A tear falls from her eye, and she quickly wipes it away.

"You are stuck with me forever," I interject.

"Maybe. Eventually, you won't need me as much. You'll find someone to share all of these special moments with."

Mom looks over at Val and smiles. "Sorry about the surprise Valerie. I didn't know Brad was bringing company." She pauses to think. "I guess I should've invited you in the first place. Well, in any case, I'm glad you're here to share this with him."

I know what she's thinking. It's what she's always thought. She really likes Val. I think she's hoping that we end up together someday. I keep telling her that Val and I are just friends; nothing more. Her response is always the same; a smile and a nod, like she doesn't believe me.

"I honestly had no idea this was happening, but thank you for letting me stay, Mrs. Pierce."

"You don't have to thank me. You are always welcomed here. Did you know that you are the first girl Brad has brought home?"

"Yes, ma'am. He mentioned that the first time around. You've raised a good boy, Mrs. Pierce. Brad is different from all of the other guys that I have met."

I've never heard Val talk about me in that way. It makes me feel ten inches taller to know she thinks so highly of me. The proud look my mom gives me lets me know she agrees with Val.

"Though I would like to, I can't take all of the credit for the way Brad turned out. I've had plenty of help, as you can see." Mom motions her arm to our family around the room. "It takes an army." She smiles brightly.

"Hi, Valerie." Gin sprouts up next to mom, drawing out Val's name with a wiggle of her brows. "It's so nice to see you again. I thought you would've gotten tired of my brother by now. He must be doing something right for a change."

"We're not a thing, but Brad has turned out to be a very good friend to me."

Poor Val. She's constantly defending herself against a relationship with me. If I were any other guy, I would probably be offended, but this is Val. Her quick defense doesn't hurt at all.

Gin smirks as she moves over to me and folds her arms around my back. "Happy birthday BP. It took you long enough to get here. Mom had me and Jeremy peeping around corners for your arrival. So, you're welcome."

"If that were your only task, I'd say you got off easy."

Gin smacks me on my arm. "Always the prude."

"Alright, children, that's enough. No bickering before cake," mom says playfully.

The party proceeds, and it's one of my better days. Everyone is together, laughing, dancing, and having a good time. Every time I spot Val, she's chatting it up with a different family member. Despite the surprise, she seems to be having a good time, and my family loves her. My dad tells me happy birthday, but other than that, we barely say anything to each other. I know eventually, I will have to find a way to move past my hurt and distrust. Right now, I just can't.

Chapter 8

Samantha

Two Years Earlier

Garrett's grades have been increasing at a steady pace since I began tutoring him. He's the perfect student. Mrs. Miller said she's impressed with our progress and feel that we should continue throughout the school year.

I think it's both a good and bad idea. Garrett's flirtatious comments have made this experience fun but difficult. I love that I get to be his sole focus for one hour, three days a week. I'm on constant alert, because one slip up and this cozy setup we have, could all turn dangerous for me. I'm well aware of how much my crush has grown for him. It's been so hard not to crawl into his arms and face rejection. Instead, I cautiously walk the line threatening to break my heart in two.

Three months.

Three months of talking, laughing, watching…

Each day Garrett's tests get easier, according to him.

My test? It gets harder with every moment that passes.

I stare outside the window at the empty field for the umpteenth time this evening. The players are beginning to gather onto the field. Inside, my mood falls. This is when

Garrett packs up his things to leave. He's a bit confusing. The way he constantly teases me, and in the blink of an eye, he's able to turn it off and leave.

"Samantha." Garrett's voice breaks through my thoughts.

I jerk my head in his direction. "Yes, Garrett?"

"I have to go, but I had a thought."

"You were thinking? How dangerous that can be," I say sarcastically. "Okay, let it out,"

Garrett chuckles while packing up his belongings.

"I think we should stop meeting here."

My heart stops beating for a few seconds. That's the way it feels. Does he not want to see me anymore?

"Hmm? I don't understand."

"This library is getting a little played out. Don't you think so?"

"It is getting stuffy in here, but I don't know of another private place we could meet."

"Football season is coming to an end soon. There won't be a need for me to stay close. We could meet at your house or mine if you're worried about your dad."

Shock.

This is not what I was expecting to come out of his mouth. Garrett wants to come to my house? I definitely wouldn't mind it, but I'm not sure how my dad would feel about it. I've never had a boy over before, and Garrett is not just any boy.

"Samantha?" Garrett is staring at me with curious eyes.

"Oh, yes. We could probably meet at my house. It's just my dad and me, but let me clear it with him first."

"Great! I better get going before coach kicks me off of the team."

He surprises me when he grabs my pen and scribbles his number on my palm.

"Give me a call later to let me know what he says."

"Okay," I say with hidden enthusiasm.

Garrett hurries off and leaves me sitting here, staring at my hand. I never want to wash my hand again. Hope begins to blossom within me. Maybe this is the start of something.

Now I just have to convince my dad to agree with this. I'm a good girl. I've never been in trouble. I don't see a reason why he wouldn't. Maybe I should get Lacy's opinion first. No, she will most definitely say no.

***

Dad should be home any minute now. I've been pacing the floor in anticipation. I entered Garrett's number into my phone for safekeeping. I also wrote it down in my diary as a precaution. I still can't believe he gave it to me. I keep staring at the screen on my phone, where I have him saved as Test. It was the only thing I could think of that wouldn't alarm my dad if he were to ever see it pop up.

I jump when I hear the door open. "Dad, is that you?" My nerves are on edge.

"How is my Sammy doing today?" Dad comes around the corner and hugs me tightly.

"Sammy had a great day, dad."

"How are your tutoring sessions going with that Garrett kid?"

"It's going good," I say, fighting to keep the excitement out of my voice. "I want to talk to you about that. Do you have a few minutes?"

"I will always make time for you, Sammy. What's on your mind?"

I can't let him know that this was Garrett's idea, or he may think there is an ulterior motive. I'll take the credit for it.

"The library has been great, but I kind of need a change of scenery for our study sessions. His grades are getting better. Although, I think he would grasp the information much faster in a more comfortable setting."

"Where are you going with this, Sammy?"

"I was wondering if it would be okay if we studied here in the afternoon." I pause to let him process an answer.

It takes a few seconds before he finally responds. "Here… in our home; while I'm at work?"

"I know what you're thinking, dad, but it's not like that with Garrett and me. We're barely even friends."

He stays silent and rubs his hand down the length of his face. A whoosh of air rushes from his lungs. This is exactly why I chose not to discuss this with Lacy. She would never go for it. She would give a hundred reasons why it's not a good idea. I've allowed myself to be sheltered and taken care of for so long that it's hard for them to let go.

"Dad? Look at me. I'm the same old Sammy. You can trust me. You, Lacy, grandma… you have all taught me well."

"Of course, I trust you. I don't know if I trust anyone else with you."

"Dad. I won't allow anyone to do anything to hurt me."

He gives me one of the hardest stares he has ever given me before. "Okay. I will agree to this, but on a trial basis, and I have to meet the young man first. Invite him over this weekend so that I can get a good look at him."

I guess this is his way of saying he wants to drill him and scare the poor guy. If that's what it takes, I'm all for it. From what I've seen, Garrett is more than capable of handling himself.

"Thanks, dad. You're the best!"

"Don't sound so disappointed," dad says sarcastically. "Nothing is set in stone yet."

I rise up on my toes to hug his neck. "I know you still have to meet him. Thank you for considering it and for trusting me. That's good enough for me."

I go to my room and call Garrett. There is a huge lump in my throat when he answers.

"Garrett here."

"Hi… Garrett, It's Samantha."

"Hey, Samantha. What's up?"

"I talked to my dad, and he wants you to come over this weekend. He wants to meet you before he makes a decision."

"Sure, I can do that. What time should I come?"

"How does eleven o'clock sound?"

"Sounds good. I'll be there."

"Okay, well, goodnight."

"Goodnight Samantha"

I hang up the phone and scream quietly into the air with the phone clutched to my chest. My weekend just got a whole lot less ordinary.

Chapter 9

Bradley

Two Years Earlier

I grab my tray of food and go to my usual spot in the cafeteria, against the side wall, and far away from the entrance. There are no windows along this side of the wall, but from where I'm sitting, I have a full view of the room and everything going on outside. I'm usually the first to arrive, followed by Timothy, Val, Ian, Brenda, and Carmen.

Timothy and Carmen are supposedly madly in love. They have known each other since pre-school. I'm not sure what is going on with Ian and Brenda. It's obvious Ian feels strongly about her, but Brenda hasn't gotten the message. She flirts with me every chance she gets. If I wanted to, I could probably snag her. She's very pretty, and any guy would be lucky to have her. I'm just not interested.

They all file in, one by one, say hello, and take their seats. Tim, Carmen, and Ian sit across from me; while Val takes the seat to my left and Brenda to my right.

Brenda touches my arm lightly, her hand lingering for a few moments. "Hi, Brad."

Ian grunts and clears his throat, but Brenda is oblivious to his reaction. Val giggles next to me.

"Hi, Brenda." I scoot closer to Val to try to put distance between us. We're all friends here, and the last thing that I want is to cause friction between us. Even though Ian and Brenda aren't together, I wouldn't want him upset because he thought I was trying to move in on his territory.

"A group of us are going to a bonfire tonight. Are you guys up for it?"

By the look on Ian's face, Brenda must have been staring at me when she asked.

"Where is it?" I ask Brenda.

"At Johnny's farmhouse out in the country."

Johnny is the kid who sponsors most of the outdoor events. His parents have a ton of land, and Johnny has them tied around his finger. He's also Brenda's older cousin by one year. So, whenever there's an event, we are always invited, and we get to hang out with the big kids.

"Tim and I are going. Aren't we baby?" Carmen asks gleefully.

Tim looks at her and nods his head. "Sure, babe."

"I'll be there," Ian says with his eyes on Brenda.

I kind of feel bad for the guy. Brenda blows him off like it's nothing.

"Are you going to be there, Brad?"

"Val and I have a standing date; so, it's up to her." I turn to look at Val. "Do you want to go with me?"

"Oh, Romeo. Where thou art, so shall I be," Val responds, clasping her hands over her heart.

A huff comes from Brenda beside me, and I fight to hold back my laughter. I know Val did it on purpose, and truthfully, I don't mind. I haven't given Brenda any indication that I like her, yet she won't give up her pursuit.

"It's settled then. We're all going. Do you need a ride, Brenda?" Ian asks, full of hope.

Brenda turns her attention to Ian, once she sees I won't take the bait. "Sure, why not?" she says, downfallen.

***

Once my mom gives me the OK to go to the bonfire, I go by and pick up Val.

The bonfire is in full swing when we get there at six-thirty. The music is blaring loud. The fire is roaring and fits for the fifty-degree weather. Some of the kids have formed a circle around the makeshift dance floor, cheering on whoever is inside. I try to get a glimpse as we approach, but the crowd is too thick.

"Hey, Brad, glad you could make it." Brenda sneaks up beside me. I hadn't even noticed her until now. "You too, Valerie," she says as an afterthought.

Val and I both say hi simultaneously.

"Who's in the circle?" I ask her, steering the attention away from me.

"That's Charlie. You know he likes to be the life of the party. Val, would you mind if I steal Brad for a dance?"

My eyes widen. She certainly doesn't waste any time. I don't mind dancing, but I don't want to do it with her. She will make more of it than it is.

"Actually, Val and I were about to…"

"No, I don't mind at all." Val cuts me off and smirks. "Go loosen him up for me. He's been tense since lunch earlier today. I'm gonna go mingle. Maybe I can find me a dance partner of my own."

"Val," I call after her.

"Have fun, Romeo."

She scurries away before I can get another word in.

"Shall we?" Brenda looks at me with so much hope in her eyes.

Dancing with Brenda turns out to be a lot of fun. For a moment in time, she made me feel like I could consider the possibility of opening my heart to someone. That thought quickly shut down when I see Ian walking towards us.

"Hey, guys. Can I cut in?" he asks.

"Sure, man. Have you seen Val around here?"

"The last time I saw her, she was headed towards the lake."

I walk away, leaving Brenda with Ian. Val is sitting by the lake with her knees tucked against her chest. I stop a few feet away and lean up against a tree. I wonder what she could be thinking about. Why is she out here alone?

I give her the space she needs while I stand watch. A soft whimper comes from her, and I begin to move closer to her. I call her name before I get too close.

"Val."

Her hands wipe at her face in a flourish. "Oh, hey. How was your dance?"

I keep walking and disregard her question. I kneel in front of her and gently place my hands on her shoulders.

"Is everything okay, Val? I thought I heard you crying." I know she was crying. I want her to confirm it herself.

She stays quiet for a few moments.

Val? You can talk to me... about anything."

"I was just feeling a little nostalgic. That's all. It's nothing to be alarmed about."

"Why are you out here by yourself? There is a bonfire not too far from here," I say to try and lighten the mood.

"I've heard." She gives me a sad smile.

I shift myself to sit down beside her, holding my hand out for her to take.

"We could have ditched the bonfire, Val. We didn't have to come. I would've much rather spent the evening alone with you. This is a rowdy bunch."

"I know that's what you say, but I... sometimes, I feel like I'm standing in the way of your happiness. Brenda is obviously into you. I didn't want you to feel like you couldn't come, just because I didn't want to."

"You are not in the way. You're my Val, and the fact that you would do that for me confirms what I knew all along," I say while staring into her eyes. "Other than Gin, you are the closest person to me. So, you could never be in the way. I don't want you to ever feel that way."

"Thank you, Brad." Val looks intently into my eyes.

"For what?"

"For being a great friend. I've never had this with anyone before."

"Well, you have it now, and I'm here for whatever you need; to lend an ear, a shoulder, a hand... I'm here."

The space around us is quiet. The water is swimming at a slow pace. The scent of the fire wafts through the air.

"It's not like anyone would notice, but we should probably get back to the bonfire."

Val's smile lights beside me. "I can think of one person who's likely missing you."

On our way back, Val asks, "Do you have any feelings at all for Brenda? Do you think she's pretty?"

I ponder over Val's question for a moment.

"I think Brenda is a very pretty girl, and I would be a fool not to like her. At the same time, she wants more than I can possibly give her. She's better off with someone who can supply her with the attention she craves. Then there's Ian, who looks at her like she's the only girl on earth. I couldn't cross that line even if I wanted to."

Val accepts my answer, and we hang around the bonfire for a little while before we leave. I managed to get a dance, and a few laughs out of her. Brenda, oddly enough, remains occupied with Ian. I caught her looking at me a couple of times, but she didn't try to engage me any further after our dance.

Val's attention is aimed at the passing trees on the way home. Whatever she's thinking about, has her in a dreary mood. She's still not ready to tell me what it is yet, and I'm not going to push her.

Chapter 10

Samantha

Two Years Earlier

Against my request, dad asked Lacy to stop by this morning. I don't know why I'm nervous about her meeting Garrett. I know that once she has a chance to meet him, she'll like him. I just have to keep my feelings for him under wraps until this introduction is over.

All of my and Lacy's previous conversations about boys have never been light. She considers that topic very important. She's told me all about the joys that a guy can bring to your life, but she has also told me about all of the pain they can cause.

Lacy has taught me right from wrong and the correct way to behave in certain situations. In her eyes, I don't think that any guy is ever going to be good enough for me. Hopefully, Garrett can change her mind because I really like him, and I hope that we could turn into something more.

"What's on your mind, Grace? You look like you're far away."

I smile when I hear Lacy's familiar voice and turn to meet her sincere eyes. "I was thinking about our conversations from before."

"And you're worried about me meeting this kid? You really like him, don't you?"

I nod my agreement. There is no need to deny what's likely written all over me. Lacy has always been able to read me very well. I should've known that this would be no different.

"Don't worry. I won't do or say anything to embarrass you, as long as he's on his best behavior." She smiles snidely.

"I appreciate everything you do for me, Lacy."

"But…?"

"There is no but. I just wanted you to know. I do have a favor to ask, though."

"Okay, what is it?"

"Can we keep this between us? Garrett doesn't know how I feel about him. I don't want to scare him off, and please don't tell dad. If he hears about this, he will never let us study here together."

"I won't tell dad, but we will have a talk about this when Garrett leaves."

I thought that Lacy would be sterner after learning of my feelings for Garrett. She's surprisingly calm about the whole thing.

"Thanks, Lacy."

"Don't thank me yet. I still have to meet him."

"Can I ask you something, Lacy?"

"Sure, you can; anything."

"With Robert, how did you feel the first time you met him?"

Lacy has that gleam in her eyes, the one she gets whenever her husband's name is mentioned. Robert spoils her, and he's the only man she sees. I hope one day to have even a fraction of the love that they have for each other. I'll be one lucky girl.

"When I met Robert, I didn't feel anything. I barely even noticed him. According to him, it took months of him coming into the bank where I work, just to get a glimpse of me through my office window; before he finally decided, that day would be the day. He made up an excuse about wanting to speak to an advisor about a loan. He made sure I was the only one in at the time."

She pauses to think.

"Thinking about it now, I should've been freaked out, but Robert wasn't a creepy guy. He was like any other patron that came into the bank. He was kind with a trusting face. He let me explain to him all about loans and such, just for the satisfaction of finally hearing my voice. When he handed me the little strip of paper with his number on it and asked me to call him some time, I should've been alarmed; any sane person would've been. Instead, I just stared at him. I studied all of him in a matter of seconds. My heart didn't skip a beat. My body temperature didn't rise. I didn't feel any way towards him, but I did think about him. There was something in his demeanor… his eyes; the way he looked at me. His courage made me want to give him a chance, and

I'm so glad I did. It's one of the best decisions I've ever made in my life."

I want that one day. I want that kind of love.

"How will I know if my feelings are real or not?"

"Feelings are tricky, Grace. They are all real. You just have to figure out whether those feelings are spent on the right person. I wish I could give you all of the answers but feelings... that's one mystery you will have to solve on your own."

The doorbell chimes, and both of us turn to look. I brush my hands down the front of my thighs and go open the door.

"Hi Garrett, come on in."

"Hi." Something about Garrett seems different today. He walks in with his hands clasped behind his back like he's nervous or thinks he may touch something he shouldn't.

"Garrett, this is my older sister Lacy. Lacy, this is Garrett Wright."

Lacy comes closer and holds out her hand for him to shake. "It's nice to meet you, Garrett. I haven't heard a whole lot about you yet. Hopefully, we can change that today."

We follow Lacy to the sitting room and find a spot. Lacy insists I sit next to her on the couch, with Garrett across from us on the love seat. Dad sits in the recliner once he joins us. He reaches over and shakes Garrett's hand.

"Nice firm handshake… I like that," dad says with a smile.

"Thank you, sir." Garrett fidgets in his chair. I've never seen him this way, not in control.

"Do you know why you are here, Garrett?"

Garrett steals a quick glance at me. I look at dad, wondering what he is up to. I knew they would try to intimidate him, but not as soon as he walked through the door. He shouldn't have to go through all of this trouble, just for a study date.

I give Garrett a sympathetic glance and mouth, 'I'm sorry.'

"Yes sir," Garrett answers, unsure of himself. "You wanted to speak with me about coming over here to study."

Dad taps his fingers on the arms of the chair. His gaze never leaves Garrett. His expression is now void of emotion.

"Aside from your study sessions, how well do you know my daughter?"

I really don't like where this line of questioning is going, but there is nothing that I can do to stop it. I know better than to interrupt dad when he's in protect mode.

"I had seen Samantha around the school. I hadn't met her until she started helping me with my math, sir. She kept to herself most of the time. I only know what she's told me since then."

Dad sits up straighter in his seat. "And what has she told you?"

"Just that she lives with her father and she has an older sister who lives nearby. She's on the swim team, but I already knew that." Garrett clears his throat.

"Did she tell you that she and her sister are the most important people in my life?"

Garrett shakes his head timidly. "No, sir, she didn't."

"Well, I'm telling you now." Dad looks at me like he knows a secret, then back to Garrett. "Are you an honest young man Garrett?"

"I would like to think so, sir."

Dad continues to grill Garrett for the next ten minutes, and all I can do is watch in silence, wishing I had never even asked. When dad is done, Lacy takes her turn, but she doesn't ask him any questions. She makes one lasting statement that we all clearly understand. *"Don't do anything to hurt her,"* is her only remark. I should be embarrassed, but I'm not. I know it's their way of expressing their love for me.

Dad agreed to us studying here when we want to. I thought Garrett would be running away screaming after all of this, but he ends up staying for lunch. It's kind of weird for me since we're not even friends. It's nice having him here, in my home with my family. It's just like I imagined it would be, except I'm not holding his hand; because it's not my hand to hold. I'm still holding on to the small bit of hope that I've always had. He didn't leave. Maybe that means something. I guess time will tell.

Chapter 11

Bradley

Two Years Earlier

Mom and dad's wedding anniversary is coming up in a few days. I can't decide if it's a joyous occasion or not. Sure, they have been together for many years, but at what cost? What exactly are they celebrating? I think that somewhere in that celebration, the entire story needs to be told. Everyone thinks that they are the perfect couple from what they see on the outside. Behind their walls, lay a much bigger picture. They get along much better these days, but I can't forget that there was a time when things weren't so great.

Dad hired one of mom's associates to come in and spruce up the backyard on the big day. All of our family and my parent's friends will be there. I've been thinking about inviting Val, but I'm not sure if she would want to come. She's not really a mix and mingles kind of girl, though she did enjoy herself at my birthday party.

Every class seems to be dragging by today. Maybe it's me wanting to get outside and enjoy the nice spring weather. I've been thinking a lot lately about Val and all of the time we spend together. I sometimes wonder if she would be open to more. Neither one of us are ready for a commitment, but maybe there is another way we can both benefit from this friendship. We already spend most of our free time together. We tell each other our secrets. Everyone else thinks we are together, except for Brenda. Why shouldn't we expand on what we have? It's just a thought that's been bugging me lately. I don't know how to bring it up to Val. I don't want to lose what we have because of my random thoughts.

The bell finally rings, signaling the end of the school day. I wait by my car for Val to join me. It never gets old watching her descend the steps of the entrance. Her head is hung low as she approaches. Her purple streaked hair swings back over her shoulder when she looks up. Her eyes shine when she spots me leaning against my car. I stare back at her, wishing we were in a position to give in. Those thoughts are always quickly shut down by the memories of my past.

"Rough day?" I ask her when she finally reaches me.

"That's one way to describe it."

"Jump in. I think we both deserve a treat after the day we've had."

"I couldn't agree more. What do you have in mind?" Val asks once we're inside.

"We haven't gone to see Jack in a while."

"But you hate the waterpark. You always say it's too crowded, and there's not enough shade."

"I know, but you love Jack's greasy burgers and fries."

"You would do that for me?" She looks at me, questioningly.

"I would. So, what do you say?" I put the car in reverse and prepare to back away.

"Who am I to turn down one of Jack's burgers and deny you the pleasure that you secretly crave?"

Jack runs a concession stand at the water park close by. Waterparks are not my favorite, but I love everything that Jack cooks up in his stand. I like to call it food for my teenage soul. I've only been there once before with Val, and she expressed to me how much she loves it there. Her mom has been taking her for years.

I cringe at the number of people gathered at the waterpark when we arrive. I remind myself that it will be worth it once I take a bite of Jack's burger and fries. Val is the happiest I've seen her all day.

"Valerie, what are you doing here on a weekday?" Jack addresses Val and cuts an eye at me. "And I see you've brought your friend back again."

"It's been a long week Jack. We need to wind down a little, and this guy practically begged me to come."

"Is that so?" Jack says with a chuckle.

"No, but it was his idea, and you know I couldn't say no."

There is a line forming behind us. Jack must finally notice and cuts the small talk. "Do you want your usual?"

"Yes. We'll both have the same thing and two of those bottled waters you have back there."

"Okay, I'll have it up in a minute."

Jack whips up our food in record time and asks Val to tell her mom hi before we leave. Luckily, we find a spot in the crowded space. There are no tables available. So, we sit under one of the few trees in the park.

We eat mostly in silence, neither one of us speaking much. I try and drown out the noise surrounding me, and Val seems to be doing the same.

"That was just what I needed today Brad, thanks."

"I have to admit, it was a great idea, but I don't like to brag," I say boastfully.

Val laughs at my playfulness.

"Val, I want to ask you something, and you are free to say no if you don't want to."

Her laughter fades as she studies me. "Okay. This must be serious. Ask away," she says, more focused now.

"My parent's anniversary is coming up in a few days, and I wondered if you would want to come with me… be my guest at the party?"

She lets out a long breath. "Is that all? I thought you were about to ask me to marry you, judging by the way you were sweating."

Maybe it's a good thing that I didn't mention the other thing. She shuts down at even the thought of commitment. A thought comes to me. This is the perfect chance to see exactly where her mind is regarding relationships.

"Would you?"

"Would I what?"

"Marry me?" I tilt my head to the side to gauge her reaction. I can see that she's shocked by my question. "I don't mean today, Val. You can relax. I just meant that if the day ever came, where you were free to love, would I be in the number? Would you consider me?"

I can feel the air thicken between us. This question stills me, just as much as it does her. I'm frightened of what her answer will be. I don't think I could ever make that kind of commitment. The fact that I even asked the question, hypothetically, has my heart racing.

She gives it plenty of thought before she finally answers. "My heart is so messed up, Brad. I honestly can't see myself getting married; ever… to anyone."

I don't know why, but I don't like her answer. Before I can respond, she continues.

"I would like to think that somewhere in another universe, there's an alternate me and you. In that universe, you would be at the top of my list." She places her hand in mine and gives it a light squeeze. "I don't know if that's the answer you were looking for, but it's all I have to give right now."

That addition makes me feel better. Her thoughts are in sync with my thoughts.

"Are you ready to get going?"

"Yeah, sure. I have a project I need to work on."

She lets go of my hand, and we stand to leave. On our way out, I realize she hasn't answered my question.

"You never gave me an answer about my parent's party."

"I would love to go. I rarely ever get to dress up and show off my girlish figure," she teases with a swish of her hips.

Things were intense for a few minutes, but she's back to her cheerful self now. I agree with Val. In another life, I would like to think that I would choose her too.

Chapter 12

Samantha

Two Years Earlier

Garrett has become more open with me since our study sessions moved to my house. We've actually become friends, and when he sees me in the hallway at school, he acknowledges me with a nod and a smile. I sometimes wonder if he's watching me as I walk away. I doubt that he is with the leeches hanging off of him, but a girl can only hope. I want to affect him the way he has affected me.

I was nervous out of my mind the very first time we were alone here. Every time I think he's going to make a move, we are interrupted by the opening of a door or the ring of a phone. That's probably a good thing, considering dad is trusting us to behave ourselves.

I scramble to get the snacks together before Garrett arrives. He comes every other day around five, like clockwork. I should be used to this by now, but the thought of having him here still gets me flustered.

It's been the same routine for the past five months. I set up snacks. He comes over. We study and we talk in between. Each time I learn something new about him that draws me even closer to him and makes me want to know more.

Garrett's favorite color is red. He likes red peppers and chicken on his pizza. He has two younger sisters, a younger brother, and two older brothers. I can only imagine what his life must be like growing up with five siblings. It would certainly keep things entertaining. He loves the game of football, but he loves to run track even more. He never joined the track team because his parents are huge football fans. His father and grandfather both played football. So, they encouraged him to focus solely on football. I wonder if TJ feels the same pressure as Garrett. I don't know if I could show as much restraint as he does. I know how hard it is to want something you can't have, and it's just within your reach.

I'm all set, and the doorbell chimes right on cue. I take a second to compose myself before I let Garrett in. I feel like the star in a coffee commercial every time I open the door and Garrett's on the other side. It's the best part of my day.

"Come on in. I was just setting up."

The way the corner of his mouth lifts to one side when he walks past me… I need a cold glass of water. A good splash over my head should do the trick. I linger near the door for a few seconds more before joining him in the living room.

Garrett is already sitting with his arm swung over the back of the couch. His legs are spread apart, inviting me to take a seat. He's watching me with hungry eyes as I grow closer. The scene is playing out nicely in my mind until I nearly trip over the throw rug beneath my feet. *So embarrassing!*

Garrett stands to help me with my near fall. "Are you okay?"

"I'm fine. You would think that I would know where everything is by now." I try to make fun of the situation before the situation makes fun of me.

He lets out a small chuckle. Then, the realization that his hand is touching my back hits me. I turn my face to look at him. He's so close I can see the tiny hairs under his chin. There is a moment between us when our eyes meet. I'm lost in his gaze until he releases his hold on me. I'm so glad I didn't do something like close my eyes and pucker up.

Garrett clears his throat and returns to his spot on the couch. "What does the teacher have in store for me today?"

"Huh?" It takes me a second to snap out of it.

"What are we working on today, teacher?"

Why does he have to be so… him? Does he know how I feel about him and thinks this is all a big joke? I need to sit down, far away from him. I settle for the recliner. It's to his right, but far enough away where I won't accidentally reach out and touch him. There's also less chance of me looking up and getting trapped in his eyes again since it's not directly in from of him.

"I thought we could focus on equations today. Once you master that, you won't need me anymore. You've been doing so well."

"Sounds good to me. Let's get started."

Well, that confirms it. He's tired of meeting with me. He's excited about the mention of him not needing me anymore. The thought of things going back to the way they before made me queasy.

When the lesson is over, Garrett lets out a long breath and takes a drink from his water bottle. I gulp at the sight of his Adam's apple bobbing with every swallow, then quickly look away. It would be a shame to get caught ogling him.

"Aah." The air oozes from Garrett's lungs. "We still have a few more sessions before this is over. I was thinking that I could take you on a date sometime. I really enjoy your company."

I'm not sure I am hearing him right, and I'm afraid to look at him. It's what I've wanted to hear from him for so long, but all I can think right now is, *why me? Why now?*

"You want to take me on a date?" It comes out more forceful than I intend.

"Yes, is it that hard to believe?"

I just stare at him in disbelief.

"You are smart and funny, and on top of that, you're beautiful."

I agree that I'm smart, and I can be funny at times, but… "You think that I'm beautiful?"

"Well yeah. I have been accused of a lot of things, but blind is not one of them."

I don't know how to respond to that. How can someone like Garrett be attracted to me? He can have any girl he wants.

Everything in me wants to say okay. My feet are itching to run to him, but I have a conscience, and it needs answers. I want to know what he sees in me; what he wants from me.

"Why," I ask him directly.

"Are you kidding me?" He eases forward in his seat. "I've always noticed you, Samantha. You are different than the other girls. I've never been intimidated by any girl until I laid eyes on you. You stole my attention from the first time I saw you."

Garrett turns his eyes away from me and continues.

"Last year on the second day of school… I knew I had never seen you before. You must have come from another school zone. I passed you in the hallway, and you didn't give me a second glance. By month six, I had decided that I would approach you. I was on my way to you during a break one day. You were sitting alone in the library looking down into a book. I had come in to check out a book for class. I remember being upset until I saw you sitting there. I thought it had to mean something. We were both there alone at the same time. Then this guy walked up and sat down beside you. He kissed you on the cheek, and you let out a quiet laugh. From where I was, you two seemed cozy. So, I checked out my book and never looked back."

I remember that day. Frederick was my closest friend in ninth grade until he moved away and had to change schools.

"Why now? What took you so long to try again?"

"The timing just feels right. I keep thinking that maybe we were put together for a reason. Every girl I meet is so hung up on my status. You… you don't seem to care. You are an anomaly to me. I like the fact that you take the time to listen when I speak, and you're not just pretending. You are the first girl that I've ever wanted to get to know because you took the time to get to know me."

Wow. I didn't know Garrett could be so deep, and all of it is directed at me. I have too many emotions running through me right now. I still can't quite believe it.

"Will you excuse me for a minute?" I ask as I stand. I go into my bathroom and stare at myself in the mirror for a few minutes. When I'm calm, I return to my seat. I still can't bring myself to answer his question. I have said yes to Garrett in my head and in my dreams more times than I can remember but to say it out loud... I don't know if I can.

"What are you thinking?"

There is another long pause before I muster up the courage to speak. "What about Cindy and Michelle?" I'm not crazy enough to think that a leech would just disappear unless you pluck it off. I refuse to be in the same frame with two other chicks. "The three of you seem awful cozy too."

"Haven't you been listening to me? Cindy and Michelle are just distractions. They help me pass the time, but the moment you tell me yes, that's all over."

"You are so confident. Do you really think it will be that easy?"

"I know it is. I've never led them to believe that we were anything more than what we are."

"Which is?" I ask with raised brows.

"Nothing. We're just a couple of teenagers that hang out from time to time."

“And they’ll be okay with you suddenly not hanging out anymore?”

“They won’t have another choice. I want to see how far you and I can go with this. That’s if you are willing to try.”

I give it some thought. I am willing but not like this. “I can’t say yes, Garrett, not until you tie up your loose ends. I don’t want to be on the receiving end of anyone’s ridicule. It’s just not me.”

Garrett’s lips curl up at the corners, and he relaxes back into the seat. He gives me a look that could melt my socks off.

“I can do that. Prepare yourself, Samantha. I’m on my way to you.”

That old familiar feeling returns to me… heat. I swallow hard. I don’t know whether to be terrified or overjoyed by this new-found knowledge. Garrett Wright wants me. I gaze at him and know that this is going to be so much fun, but I can get in so much trouble with Garrett. What will my dad think? What will Lacy think?

Chapter 13

Bradley

Two Years Earlier

Why do people have parties anyway? What's the point? It's your special day. You spend tons of money. You get all dressed up and invite a bunch of people over, just to parade around for a couple of hours, to show them how happy you are. Why can't you do that without all of the add-ons?

There's a huge tent set up in the backyard, decorated well enough for a king and queen. They even laid down the red carpet leading inside the elegantly decorated tent. Tables and chairs are placed in rows around the space, covered in white cloth with mint green and silver trimmings. The vases are filled with purple calla lilies. A dance floor is set up in the center floor, with a small staging area up near the front. It's beautiful.

I don't care for parties, but mom is happy. Her smile is real. Any day when I can see my mom's smile is worth the hassle.

The worst part about today is the dress pants, and button-down shirt mom made me wear. I feel so uncomfortable and out of sorts. The best thing about today is walking up my driveway looking surprisingly comfortable in the blue knee-length dress she has on. I notice that she's changed the streaks in her hair to a dark blue to match her dress. I wonder if she knows how beautiful she is.

"Drool much?" Gin sneaks up behind me at the front door.

It's probably a good thing that she startled me. It gives me a chance to clear my mind of all of the naughty thoughts I was thinking. "I'm not drooling. It's called admiring."

Gin steps beside me. "She is beautiful. Have you two ever talked about trying out the relationship thing together?" Gin holds her hands, palms up, and moves them like a balance scale. "I mean… you're a guy. She's a girl. You spend so much time together."

"No, we haven't. We are just friends, Gin." I have thought about it, but I won't let Gin know, and after Val's reaction the other night, I can't tell her either.

I plaster on a smile as Val reaches the door.

"Hi, Val." Gin gives her a gracious greeting and gives me a sly look. It's never good when she does that.

I give her a subtle nudge to warn her away. Gin, being the person that she is, ignores me. She slides her arm between Val's and pulls her inside.

"Hi, Val. I'm sorry about her," I say, nodding my head at Gin. "She doesn't know how to act when company comes over."

"I do too," Gin wines. "Val, you and I should have a girl's talk sometime. Maybe we can give each other some pointers and exchange stories. It has to get dull hanging around this dud. He is such a party pooper."

"I would like that. Though, I don't know what pointers I could possibly give you," Val responds.

"Don't worry. There is plenty we can talk about and as for pointers…" Gin leaves it to the imagination, her brows wiggling up and down.

"I think that's enough for now. Can I have my girl… my friend back now, Gin? I'm sure Jeremy is wondering where you ran off to."

Both sets of eyes snap to mine. Val inhales a breath, and Gin's smile is still as sly as ever. It's the first time that I've called Val my girl. I don't know what I was thinking. I blame it on the dress and Gin for planting those thoughts in my head.

"My pleasure," Gin says, proudly. She's obviously accomplished what she came to do.

I'm afraid to look at Val, fearing that she may turn around and walk back out of the door. I've never been in a more awkward moment before now. I chance a glance at Val. Her cheeks are flushed, but she shows no signs of flight. Maybe she didn't catch my slip up.

"Your girl, huh?"

"I didn't mean it that way, Val." I pause to try to think of a good excuse, why I would say something like that. I decide to play it cool. "Technically, you are my girl, and I'm your guy. It just sounds out of place when it's said out loud for others to hear."

Val covers her laugh with her hand. "It's okay, Brad. I kind of like being your girl." She pushes her shoulder into my side, playfully.

"You clean up nicely," I say as I blatantly check her out from head to toe.

"You don't look so bad yourself, guy." She looks around the room. "Where is everyone? Am I too early?"

"No, you're not too early. Most of the guests have already gone out to the tent. I figured I would stay inside and direct everyone. I was mostly waiting for you to arrive. The crowd out there is kind of thick."

"And I know how much you don't like large amounts of people. Are your parents around? I wanted to say hi and give my congrats, just in case I don't get to later."

I take Val to see mom first. Mom always acts as if Val is one of her own. We visit dad next. I don't say much. Val does most of the talking. I want to tell him that I'm happy for him and mom. I want to hug my dad or, at the very least, shake his hand. Things have gotten a little better between us, but we're still not there yet.

The party starts right on time. They renew their vows during the ceremony. To look at them, one would think that they were newlyweds. They look so happy, so in love.

Val sniffles next to me. I try not to pay too much attention. I don't want her to be embarrassed.

I never understood why people cry at weddings. I'm not one of those overly emotional souls. I was once until everything changed. Now I'm just a shell with half of a heart.

It's not long before dinner is served, the cake is cut, and the dancing begins. Val and I dance to a couple of upbeat songs after my parents first dance. When the music slows, we both stop and stare at each other. I've held Val in my arms before but never in a slow dance. I hold my hand out to her, and she takes it. The closer she gets to me, the more my nerves tingle. Cheek to chest, we sway to the music. It feels… good, comfortable, right, a little too good. Parts of me are coming to life that I'm not sure Val wants to feel.

Val holds her head up off of my chest and looks into my eyes. There's something in her eyes that I've not seen before.

"Do you want to go outside? I need some fresh air," she says hurriedly.

"Yeah, I could use some air too. It's getting stuffy in here."

It's only a few steps to the exit, but it feels like miles. I imagine this is what it must feel like to take the walk of shame.

The sun has already set, and the moon winks at us with a tenth of an eye. We take a seat on the swing hanging from the old oak tree in the backyard. This entire evening has taken an unexpected turn. We sit quietly, staring ahead.

"Brad."

"Val"

We both speak in unison.

"You go first," she says to me.

How do I begin? Should I feel guilty for being attracted to my best friend? "I don't really know what to say. I didn't mean to react to you that way in there. I tried, but I couldn't stop it. Seeing you like this tonight opened up a wormhole. I'm so sorry, Val."

Val places her fingers over my lips. The feel of her hand does nothing to help things. Her fingers are soft and careful as they move across my lips.

"Val."

"It's okay, Brad. There's nothing to apologize for. I feel it too. I've felt it for a while now, the pull between us. Maybe…"

A grain of hope blossoms in me at the word… maybe.

"Maybe we can explore whatever this is. We both want the same things, right? Neither one of us is capable of being in love. We both want simple. We both shy away from commitment. So, maybe we can just be. I can be your girl, and you can be my guy; no strings attached. What do you think?"

"I could live with that. Let's just enjoy the next two years together before we go off to college."

Val gets quiet, and her eyes tear up. "Did I say something wrong, Val?"

"No. You always know the right things to say. I need to tell you something, Brad."

In my experience, nothing good ever came after that statement.

"My mom has been thinking about moving away from here. She wants to start over fresh somewhere new. She's tired of being constantly reminded of our past. She assured me she'll try to wait until I graduate, but I don't know if she will hold on that long. I can tell she's not happy here. Anyway, I don't know how long this thing with us will last. If you don't think…"

"No." I cut her off. The truth is, I don't care how long it will last. I just want the memories of us. She's the closest I'll ever get to love. "I don't care. We have now, and that's all that matters."

Val surprises me with a kiss on my lips. Her lips linger on mine. It's warm. It's sweet. It's real, and it's our first kiss, one that I will never forget.

Chapter 14

Samantha

Two Years Earlier

I don't know if I'll ever get used to the dirty looks from Cindy and Michelle. It's funny how they didn't know my name before. I was irrelevant, just a blip on their map. It seems that my being is all they know now.

Garrett was serious about getting to know me. Within a week's time, he had distanced himself from the leeches. They were not happy at all, especially when they found out why.

Things started out slow at first. The hardest part for me was telling dad and Lacy. They weren't too surprised. They knew it would happen eventually. My dad stressed to Garrett again how important I am to him. I don't know how it affected Garrett, but it sure would scare the crap out of me if I were in his shoes.

Lacy was tasked with the fun part. She sat us both down and reminded us of what we already know. The good old birds and bees talk. It was so embarrassing, but I would do it all over again for this shot with Garrett.

We've been dating for a few weeks now, and Garrett is the sweetest boyfriend I never had. He is everything that I thought he would be.

It's strange having someone hold my hand on the way to class and carry my books to my locker. There is so much to like about being Garrett's girl, but being Garrett's girl comes with a price. Everywhere we go, the popular girls stare at us like we are Oreos and day-old milk. I guess they all want to know the same thing I did in the beginning; why me? The guys could care less. I hear whispers when we pass the leeches, but it doesn't matter. None of it matters. I'm finally living out my fantasy.

It's the end of the school day, and I can't wait to get out of here. I jump when a pair of arms wrap around me from behind. I haven't gotten used to Garrett's open displays of affection yet. I find myself looking around to see who is watching us. I don't know what normal behavior is for a new couple. Garrett is my first of everything. Is this what's supposed to happen this early on? Am I supposed to want his touch as much as I do?

"I missed you," Garrett whispers softly in my ear.

I turn around to face him. "It's only been a couple of hours, Garrett. I don't think that counts as enough time to miss me."

"Any time spent away from you counts."

I close my locker and turn back to him. "That's really sweet, Garrett, but it's such a line. You don't have to feed me lines to keep me interested. What did you say I was?" I tap my finger along my chin. "Different… that's the word."

"Hey, it wasn't a line. I did miss you, and in case you forgot, this is all new to me. The old Garrett is gone."

"Gone? Don't be silly. There are some things I really like about old Garrett."

He leans forward. His mouth is barely touching my ear. "Maybe you should tell me all about those things."

"Maybe I should," I said daringly. I'd forgotten we were in the hallway under prying eyes. Garrett has a way of making me forget.

He steps back, producing that cocky smirk that I like. "Later for sure. Right now, I want to take you somewhere."

I call dad to let him know that I won't be home right away. He's okay with it. For some reason, he trusts us together.

I don't know where we are going until we get there. Garrett parks the car on the side of the road and grabs a bag from the back seat when we get out. He drops enough change into the parking toll for four hours.

"Where are we going," I ask him.

"You'll see. Come on." He grabs my hand and guides us toward the huge mound near the beach. He pulls a blanket from the bag, lays it on the ground at the peak of the mound and motions for me to sit. "We're just in time."

"The beach? Why are we here, Garrett?"

I follow his eyes to the setup on the beach. The sun is just beginning to descend from the sky, providing the perfect backdrop for the wedding that's about to take place.

"A wedding," I say in awe. I turn to look at Garrett for a moment. Does he like weddings? This is a side of him I didn't know he possessed. "How did you know about it?"

"My oldest brother is a photographer. That's him down there with the camera." Garrett points to a guy wearing khakis and a polo shirt. I can't tell if he looks anything like Garrett from where we are.

"Do you do this often… attend stranger's weddings?"

"Not often, just when I need to be knocked down off of my pedestal." He grunts out a laugh. "The attention gets to be too much at times. I come here to think. There is something about a wedding that grounds me; reminds me of what I want to have one day."

And he thought bringing me with him was a good idea? Does he know what this could possibly hint at in a girl's mind... my mind? I push the thoughts of this one day being him and me away, knowing that wasn't his intention. He obviously just wanted to share something he enjoys with me.

"Did your brother ever play football?" I ask, changing the subject.

Garrett laughs at the thought. "Yeah, he did, but he was not good at it. Preston is not the athletic type. My parents tried to force him into it. So, he did his worst, and they kicked him off of the team eventually. This is his passion. He's good at finding the beauty in everyday things and capturing the true essence of people."

Just then, the bride emerges from a distance and walks the sand towards her groom. This is the first time I've ever seen a wedding on the beach. I can barely see their faces, and I can't hear the words spoken, but their body language speaks volumes. It's the most romantic thing I've ever seen. It's like watching an opera play out, where you have no idea what's being sung, but you can feel it in your bones. I'm fighting to hold in the tears that are threatening to fall. Neither of us says a word until it's over.

"That was breathtaking," I say.

Garrett watches me with curious eyes. "I'm glad I could share it with you."

He pulls me close to him and gazes deep into my eyes. I know by his look that he's going to kiss me. His arms circle around me, and I make a choice to give in to him. Our first kiss is everything, nothing like I thought it would be and so much more than I imagined. I lay my head on his shoulder and quietly revel in the after-effects.

After the wedding is over, we stay and watch the sunset. Then Garrett drives me home.

I close the front door and lean against it. Tonight, was perfect. I sigh deeply and push off the door. I stop in my tracks at the sight of dad sitting on the couch, realizing he just witnessed my reaction.

"Dad. You startled me." One more thing to add to my list of embarrassing moments.

"Hey, Sammy. Looks like you had a good time."

I thought he would be upset by me coming home after dark. "I did. Garrett took me to a wedding on the beach."

"That explains the look," dad says with a light chuckle.

"What look?"

"The, I'm living in a fairytale look. Weddings tend to do that kind of thing."

"That's… I'm not… I don't…" I don't know what to say. Dad is right. I do feel like I'm living a fairy tale.

"I want you to have fun, Sammy. Just be careful. Hearts don't mend as easily as they break."

I give my dad a big hug and go to my room. I think about what my dad said. Then I think about Garrett. I have seen his softer side, a side of him that no one else has seen. I am willingly giving him a part of me that few others know; my heart. My heart is fragile, and I'm not sure if I could withstand it if Garrett were to break it.

Chapter 15

Bradley

One Year Earlier

It's that time of year when all of the girls in school are running around like a chicken with their necks cut off. The infamous prom is coming up in about a month. Val and I haven't discussed it, but I feel like I should ask her to go with me. I think it's like a rite of passage thing for girls. I could be mistaken, though. I have no experience with these things.

Gin has been preparing for this day for months. She and Jeremy are all set for the big night. She has her dress and shoes with all of the other trimmings, and Jeremy has his matching tux. She brags that the only thing left for her to do is her hair and nails and says I need to get moving if Val and I are going. I don't see what the big deal is. If it were up to me, I'd put on a black suit and tie, and Val could wear whatever. It's one night, and when it's all said and done, what I really want is to be with Val.

Val told me that her mom had made a decision about moving this past week. She told her she would let her finish out this year, but after that, they would be gone. The two years we were hoping for has been reduced to only one, and that one is quickly coming to an end. I don't know how to feel about that. Val and I have grown closer than ever since the night we decided to just be. I'll be losing my best friend. I'm going to make the best of the time we have left, while I still can. If taking her to prom is what she wants, I'm willing to pay the price.

"How would you feel about going to prom with me?" I ask Val on the drive home from school.

"I hadn't really thought about it. My mind has been bogged with thoughts of moving away. Why? Did you want to go?"

"It's not at the top of my list of things to do, but I think it would be fun. If nothing else, it will be entertaining to watch everyone else. It'll give you an excuse to get up close and personal with me." My brows twitch at the thought.

"I don't need an excuse for that unless you have some new rule I'm not aware of. I think it could be fun too. I would need a dress, and you'd need something to match my attire. It doesn't have to be anything fancy, though. The basics will suit me just fine. I can't imagine spending all of that money for one night."

"I was just thinking that same thing, but I didn't know your thoughts on the matter."

"Well, you know what they say about great minds."

"Any particular colors you want to wear?" I ask her.

"What about black and white. That should be easy enough to find."

I pull up outside Val's house and turn off the engine.

"Would you like to come inside for a while? My mom won't be home for another hour or so."

"Are you sure that's such a good idea? Your mom might freak out if she comes home and finds me here. She's only met me once before." I use that as my excuse. In reality, her mom is the least of my worries.

"Come on. It will be fine. My mom knows how cautious I am with people. We have an unspoken understanding. If I trust you, then she trusts you. She knows that I would never let just anyone get too close."

I hesitate before getting out of the car. Trust… I'm not sure if I trust myself to be alone with her. I've kissed Val before, and each time it gets harder not to want more. "If you think it's okay, then sure. I have to warn you, though."

"About what?"

"Kissing me the way you do. With no one to stop us, things may get dangerous."

Val laughs at my antics. "Come on, lover boy. Nothing is going to happen that I don't want to happen."

Val has a way with words, and I never can tell if she's serious when she speaks about these things. I begin to wonder, *what does she want to happen?* I know what I want, but it's probably best to keep things simple, especially now that she's leaving in a few months.

We get out, and Val walks ahead of me, switching her hips along the way. She glances back over her shoulder, blows a kiss and winks. It's one of the special moments that Val and I share. She's not an over-affectionate girl. So, when she does things like that to me, I'm more turned on than I probably should be.

Once we're inside, I stand by the door feeling uncomfortable, not knowing what to do next.

"Don't just stand there. It's okay to step out of the headlights deer." Val snickers at her own joke, and I laugh along. She has a weird sense of humor. Most of our friends don't get her as I do.

I ease further inside. Val motions for me to follow her to the kitchen. I sit down on one of the bar stools. I try to keep my breathing even and in short spurts to fend off as much of her sweet scent as possible. It doesn't help when she stands right next to me.

"Would you like a drink or a snack?"

Val walks toward the fridge, and I breathe a sigh of relief. I don't know how to do this; how to be… here with her alone. There is a war inside of me and a pull between us even stronger that has absolutely nothing to do with love. That's the worst kind of pull and the best… the kind where there's no risk involved, no chance of heartbreak, no mixed feelings, yet the emotion is so thick, it can't even be cut with a knife.

"I could use a drink; the colder, the better," I say strained. "A sandwich would be nice too if you have it." Maybe if I eat something, it'll take some of the hunger away.

"Coming right up," Val sings. She knows what I like, so I don't need to tell her what to whip up.

Val makes me a sandwich and slides it over to me with an extremely cold fruit punch bottle. She makes herself the same and sits down next to me. We eat mostly in silence. I help her clean up the mess when we're done and return to my seat on the barstool. Val comes to stand between my legs and places her hands on my shoulders. My hands immediately go to her waist.

"Now that we are well fed, we should probably discuss the details of this prom thing a little more. It's not far away, so we don't have much time." Her hand slides down to lay flat against my chest. "I was thinking that I could wear a plain white dress and try to find some kind of black accessory to go with it."

My thumbs find the space between her shirt and jeans and make small circles. "And I could wear a black suit and tie with a white shirt. I'll spring for a black corsage for you." My conscious mind knows that I'm speaking, but there's another part of me screaming louder than ever before. Her skin feels amazing.

Val steps closer to me. She's only a hair away from my treasure. Her breath hisses over my skin. I can't take it any longer. I pull her into me. My lips skate down the length of her neck and around to her lips. When her lips touch mine, I feel a jolt of something wicked. She kisses me back with need. As much as I want to go further, I know we shouldn't. I slow the kiss and pull away, placing my forehead on hers.

"I should probably go, Val, before your mom comes home."

"Are you sure?" she asks me breathily.

"No, but if I stay…" If I stay what? There are so many ways that I could finish that sentence. If I stay, I'll kiss you again; more passionately than ever before. If I stay, I'll touch you in places I've never seen. If I stay, we'll do grown-up things that we can never come back from. If I stay, I'll hold you like a young man who's not incapable of love, except I am incapable. It would be selfish of me, and it wouldn't be fair to Val to take away something so precious. She may change her mind one day and fall for someone perfect. "I can't stay Val," I say softly into her ear. I kiss the temple of her head and back away.

She looks disappointed, and it hurts me that I made her feel this way. "Okay. Well, I'll call you later to go over the rest of the details."

Val leans over and places a small peck on my lips. I take a deep breath once I'm in my car. My body screams at me, but I know that I've made the right decision.

Chapter 16

Samantha
One Year Earlier

Things with Garrett and I are much smoother now that the shock has finally worn off. People barely pay attention anymore. I'm just a girl who's crazy about a guy. Garrett's football season this school year has been great, and I was his fiercest cheerleader at every game.

Swim practice will soon be starting. I can't say that I'm too excited about it; the early mornings and weekend competitions. It's like everything is different now. It amazes me how much my passion has changed for something that I felt so strongly about before. My direction has shifted, and my heart now burns for something new. I won't quit, though. I have to see it through. I can't let my family down.

Aside from swim, Garrett and I have been preparing for prom. He has been a good sport about the whole thing from the moment he asked me to go with him. He even helped me pick out our colors. He's that kind of guy. He likes to be involved in all of the decision makings where our relationship is concerned.

I've been fitted for my dress, and Garrett has reserved his tux. Keeping with the fairy tale I have in my head, my dress will be a surprise to Garrett on prom night. The color is the only detail that he knows. I can't wait to see the look on his face when he sees me in it.

Garrett is anything but predictable, but there is one thing that I can count on daily. The way he creeps up behind me and wraps his arms around me doesn't change. I've gotten used to his daily hall wraps. Instead of being startled, like in the beginning, I lean into him now. I hope there never comes a day when I'm missing his touch. I've never felt a feeling so right.

Over the past year, Garrett has spoiled me into thinking that there's no one greater for me. He has wormed his way into my heart in all of the best ways.

My eyes close and my head falls back onto Garrett's shoulder when his arms enfold around me. I breathe him in without turning around. His breath on my neck is warm and inviting. I wonder how or if it can get any better than this.

He speaks softly into my ear. "Hey, babe. I missed you," he says, spouting that same phrase he whispers to me every day.

I smile and turn in his arms to face him. "I missed you too."

"How about we get out of here and go somewhere with a little more privacy?"

"When you say privacy, how private are we talking?"

"I was thinking that we could hang out at my house today. We'll have the place to ourselves without interruption."

Our make-out sessions have been really heated lately. We've been skirting around the elephant in the room for weeks now. I want to take things to the next level with him, but I'm not sure if I'm ready. Though Garrett has been great and he's assured me I'm his one and only, I still have that small speckle of doubt. My fear is that he will realize what a huge mistake he's made if we go through with it. I'm also afraid of losing him if we don't.

I keep up my air of confidence, hiding my insecurities behind my smile. "I think that can be arranged."

Half of the time, I don't know what I'm saying until it's already out of my mouth, like now. The old me would have never agreed to visit with a guy alone. The old me would have made up some excuse. The new me is so entranced by Mr. Wright that I can barely see my next move before I make it.

***

Garrett unintentionally lied to me. When we arrived at his house, his mom and younger siblings were home. Surprisingly, it didn't bother me too much. I was kind of relieved that we were not alone. It gave me a chance to think about what I want.

Garrett went up to change and left me in the company of his family. Despite knowing that she had a part in forcing Garrett to play football, I like his mom. She reminds me of one of those ladies that live for the PTA. I'd be willing to bet that she's the president. She looks like she loves to be in charge of everything.

Garrett's little brother, Henry, didn't pay much attention to me. He said hi and kept it moving. His sisters, on the other hand, decided to engage in a staring war with me. They giggle their way through it, and in the end, I win the war. They are identical twins. So, I can't tell which one is Carly and which one is Jane.

Garrett told me the story behind them and how they came about. His mom always wanted a little girl, but she ended up with four boys. She had given up and had her tubes tied after having Henry. Less than three years later, she found out she was pregnant with twin girls.

"Carly, Jane… leave the poor girl alone. I'm sure she doesn't want you staring at her like that." Their mom's voice cuts through before we can begin another match.

She smiles at me politely. "Don't mind them. Sometimes they forget their manners."

"They're no problem at all, Mrs. Wright," I respond in the sweetest voice I can muster up.

It's just as awkward as all of the other times I was here. I never know what to say to his mother. She's kind of intimidating.

She turns her attention to the girls for a moment. "Girls, go upstairs and get your brother. We'll be leaving soon."

I straighten at the thought of them leaving. That means Garrett and I will be alone. Mrs. Wright's sudden expression change has me worried.

"You and my son have been dating for about a year now. Is that correct?" she asks me directly.

"Yes, ma'am." I wonder where this conversation is headed. What was so important that she had to excuse the twins?

"You do realize that Garrett will be going away to college in another year, don't you?"

"Yes, ma'am. I do."

"My son is…" She pauses to think about her next words. "He's a young man Samantha, with a bright future in front of him. Both of you are. You don't need to be tied to one person at such a young age. Have the two of you discussed what will happen when you graduate from high school?"

I take a moment to think about her question. I've been so wrapped up in the fairy tale, that I didn't stop to really think about it. I always figured we had time. I pictured Garrett and I going off to the same school once we graduate. His mom makes a good point, but it's none of her business. I wonder if she's said anything to Garrett about this. What are his thoughts about our future?

"We haven't discussed anything past going to prom in a few weeks."

I hear little voices getting closer to us, along with Garrett's tenor. They must be on their way back downstairs. Garrett's mom stands and pats me on the shoulder lightly.

"You should probably talk about it. I'm not trying to discourage you. I just don't want to see anyone get hurt. Just think about what I said and talk to my son."

I think to myself. S*he surely has a glowing way of showing encouragement. That certainly was not her approval.* How do I bring this up with Garrett? Should I even bother?

I'm in a sour mood after his family leaves. I don't know what to do. I can't stop thinking about what his mom says.

"Hey babe, is something bothering you? You seem miles away. You were fine until…" Garrett stops speaking mid-sentence. "Did my mom say something to you?"

"It's nothing. She's just looking out for you."

He scoots closer to me on the couch and takes my hand in his. "What did she say? It must have been something awful to put you in this kind of mood."

Instead of telling him what his mom said, word for word, I decided to just come right out and ask the questions on my own. "Garrett, have you thought about what you're going to do after high school is over? Do you see a future for you and me?"

Garrett sits back on the couch and pulls me with him. "Of course, I've thought about it. I know that I'm going to college, but I haven't decided where yet. I guess that will depend on whether or not I get a scholarship." His lips touch my temple, and his arms wrap around me tighter. "As for you and me, I see lots of stuff happening in our future. You, me, a little Garrett somewhere down the line."

To hear him speak of having a child with me boosts my mood. Maybe his mom is wrong. Maybe we aren't too young. We both want the same things, and I'm sure we can make us work, as long as we're on the same page.

"A little Garrett? Really? You've never mentioned kids before." I raise my head in his direction.

"You've never asked." He shrugs his shoulders. "Listen, babe. My mom has this idea of me in her head. I've been over this with her before, and she refuses to back down and let me map out my own future. For now, I'm letting her have her way, but eventually, she won't be able to tell me what I can and cannot do. Now… there are much better things I'd rather be doing than talking about my mother."

Our eyes lock, and Garrett moves in for a simmering kiss. His hand holds the side of my face. My eyes fall close at the first taste of Garrett's lips. This thing between us… it's much more than a teenage crush. If I wasn't sure before, I am now. I love Garrett Wright.

Chapter 17

Bradley

One Year Earlier

I run my hand down the front of my suit jacket as I take one final look in the mirror. I think to myself. *You clean up nice.* I didn't go out and purchase a tux like I suspect everyone else did. I opted for a simple black suit, just like Val & I planned. I won't be picking Val up in a limo either. Gin offered to share her and Jeremy's limo, but I declined. I would much rather be able to go where ever we want to when prom is over. So, we're taking my car.

"You look nice, BP." Gin startles me from my doorway. I turn to face her. I should've closed the door. "I still can't believe you took the plunge and asked Val to go. You hate crowds." She walks in a little further.

"This is a different kind of crowd, and I had a feeling she would like to go." I shrug.

"Sounds like love to me," Gin teases.

"Not the kind of love that you think. I love Val, but…" How do I explain this to Gin? Do I even need to explain? "Val and I have an understanding. Neither of us is built that way. I love her, and she loves me. It's not like with you and

Jeremy, though." I tell Gin just about everything, but I feel exposed telling her this. I've never expressed my concerns about love with anyone but Val.

"What are you saying, BP?" Gin looks to be concerned.

I blow out a deep breath. "Nothing… it's nothing. I just want to have a good time tonight." I notice that she's not ready yet. "Why aren't you dressed? Have you changed your mind about going?"

"Absolutely not. I wouldn't miss this for anything. I just need to slip on my dress and shoes. It should only take me ten minutes, tops."

"I should probably get going. I guess I'll see you guys there."

"BP, wait." Gin stops me when I take a step towards the door. "I know we haven't talked as much as we used to lately, but I want you to know that you can always come to me. Just because I have Jeremy, it doesn't mean that I'm not available to listen. I was your sister first. That's never going to change."

Gin is sweet when she wants to be. This is one of those moments. I nod my head and give her a hug before I leave the room. I haven't told her that Val is leaving yet. I may have to hold her to her words soon.

Mom stops me at the front door. "Son, I know you're not trying to sneak out before I get my picture."

"We're taking pictures at prom, mom."

"I know, but it's not the same. I want to capture your before and after as well. Turn around and let me look at you."

I know there is no way she will let me leave until I do as she asks. I make a full circle and end in a pose with my hand clutching the lapel of my suit.

"You are so handsome, son." She pats my cheek gently. "Hold that pose for a minute." Her smile beams as she raises the camera and snaps picture after picture."

"Mom, I really should be going."

"I know, I know. Have a good time tonight and tell Valerie I'm expecting pictures."

"I will, mom. Love you." I give her a hug and a kiss on her cheek before I go.

***

I don't know why I'm nervous. It could be that Val and I haven't shared a kiss or haven't been completely alone since the day I walked out of her home. Things weren't awkward between us after that. We still talk every day. We still laugh. We still keep secrets. She's still my best friend.

I ring the doorbell and wait. My foot taps against the cemented porch. I'm about to ring the bell again when the door opens.

Val smiles widely at me. "Hey, handsome."

"Hey yourself, beautiful." Val looks lovely in her white knee-length white dress. The dress is fitted up top with spaghetti straps adorning her shoulders. It flanks out from her waist down, like a wilted flower. She has her hair pinned up tonight. It's the first time I've ever seen Val with totally black hair. Her heels make her taller than she truly is. Her eyes almost match mine.

"Are you ready to party?" she asks me.

"Ready when you are." I hold up the corsage I picked out for her. "There's one thing missing from your ensemble, not that you need it." My eyes roam the length of her. She holds out her wrist for me to slide it on. "Perfect."

"Let me just grab my clutch. I'll be right back."

We make small talk on the ride over to prom. Val is in a much better mood these days, and I wonder if it's a cover-up to hide how she really feels. I know deep down that she doesn't want to leave, but I also think there is a part of her that feels the same as her mom. She's never told me exactly what happened. All I know is it has something to do with her absent father. Is she going to miss me as much as I will her? I haven't asked where they are going. Knowing will only make it all too real. I'm not ready to let go yet.

The venue is already packed when we get there. The school really went all out for prom this year. There is valet parking for those of us that drove and a separate section for the limousines. Inside, the lights are dim, except for the photo booth area set up out front. Val and I take pictures first; one less thing we'll have to worry about later. There are circular tables set up around the room, with four place settings on each table. The music is pumping throughout the space. Hardly anyone is on the dance floor that's surrounded by tables on the center floor. There's a lot of mingling going on. I don't see Gin and Jeremy anywhere. She's probably going to show up fashionably late. The thought makes me laugh.

"What has you so tickled? Is there something on my face?" Val asks.

"I was thinking about Gin showing up late. She likes to make an entrance."

"I can imagine." Val looks around quizzically. "What do people do at these things anyway? Is there like an itinerary we have to follow or something?"

"I have no idea. I guess we can find a table."

We sit down in silence for a while, listening to upbeat music. Gin finally makes her entrance fifteen minutes later. She hangs on Jeremy's arm as they make their way around. The room is nearly packed when the music fades away. Donna Hendricks, the senior class president, steps up to the microphone and gives a small speech, after which she goes over the plans for tonight.

Gin and Jeremy sit at the table with us. Dinner is served first, followed by dancing. When Val and I dance, it's just her and me. Everything else fades away. It's not long before that old familiar feeling creeps up on me. I have to shut my mind off and think about something else. It's either that or back away slowly.

We take a short break for the other heads of the class to speak. None of what they are saying has anything to do with us since we still have to suffer through another year of school. Most of it goes in one ear and out the other. I'm relieved when they finish up so I can get back to holding Val.

As we sway to the music, all sorts of thoughts flow through my mind. I think about the first time we met, the first time I held her in my arms, the first time we kissed… I think about all of the secrets we've shared, the laughter, the sadness… I think about what a great person Val is and about the crap life she's been dealt. I think about her leaving me and how I will feel when she's gone. The thought makes me hold her even tighter. A few more weeks and my greatest distraction will only be a memory.

Val lifts her head from my shoulder to gaze into my eyes. "Do you want to get out of here?" she asks softly.

"I thought you'd never ask," I reply. Tonight was great, but right now, I just want to take her away from here. I want to be selfish. I want her all to myself.

I let Gin know that we are leaving. She's so wrapped up in Jeremy. I don't know if she heard me or care. Instead of spending the night out, as I imagine most of the other prom-goers will do, Val and I go back to her house and spend the next two hours watching standup comedy. It's probably what we should've done all along. This is our idea of fun.

I watch Val from the corner of my eye, laughing at the comedian on television. I take a mental picture and file this moment away. I don't know if I can get used to missing that laugh.

Chapter 18

Samantha

One Year Earlier

Lacy came over tonight to help me get ready. I don't know what I would do without her. She's just finished my hair, and she insisted on doing my makeup too. Earlier today, she took me to the nail salon for a mani-pedi. I feel like such a princess.

The closer the time gets for Garrett to arrive, the more butterflies flutter in my stomach. Tonight has to be perfect. I've waited for this day for so long. It's been a part of my waking dream since the first time I saw Garrett.

I slip on my dress, and Lacy helps me with my zipper. I'm pleased with my choice as I stare at myself in the mirror. Lacy looks over my shoulder, smiling from ear to ear. I see my mother in her eyes. A tear rolls down my cheek at the thought.

Lacy quickly grabs a tissue to dab at the lone tear. "Oh, Grace… You're going to make me cry. I can't believe my little sister is all grown up. You look like an angel."

"Thanks, Lacy. I wish mom were here with us."

"So do I, but you know what? Even though she's not, I believe she's watching. We can't see her, but she will always be here." Lacy places her palm over my heart. "She would be so proud of the young woman that you've become."

"You think so?"

"I know so. Now… we have to finish getting you ready. So, no more crying or you'll ruin your makeup."

"I can't make any promises. I'm so ready for this, and my emotions are all over the place."

"I know a little something about how you feel," Lacy smirks like she remembers something. "I was where you are once. I didn't go to my prom, but I had a huge crush on this boy named Lance when I was in high school. Of course, I never got the guy but the feelings he elicited inside of me… He was two years older than I was, and he had a girlfriend. I never stood a chance, but it didn't stop me from hoping. He bumped into me in the hall one day at school and knocked my books to the floor. When I bent to pick them up, he helped me. Our eyes locked, and I was struck from that point on. He was always so nice to me despite our age difference. We became friends, but it never went any further than that. We lost touch after he graduated." Lacy sighs. "I guess it's a good thing or I may not have met Robert."

I love Lacy's stories. She doesn't offer them up often. So, I pay close attention when she does. Her stories always lead to a message. I know she's trying to tell me something in her own way.

"Before meeting Robert, did you ever think about looking him up?" Lacy never brought any guys around when I was growing up. I wonder if I'm the reason. If it weren't for me, would she have pursued a relationship before she did?

"Of course, I did, but I knew I couldn't put in the time and effort it would take. I had you and dad to think about. Whenever the thought crossed my mind, I would always think about something mom used to say to me when I was younger. She would say to me, *baby girl, don't go looking for love. Let love find you. Remember that what is meant to be will be.* Lance was never meant to be in my life forever, Grace. He was just there for that moment in time to fill a space."

"Garrett is a sweet boy, and at this point in your life, you feel like there is no one who could ever take his place. Be careful with him, Grace. Sometimes it takes guys a little longer to truly figure out what they want."

Deep down, I know Lacy means well, but I know Garrett would never hurt me. I nod and refocus on getting ready.

***

My heart is beating out of my chest when Garrett picks me up. Both Lacy and dad tell me to have a great time. Dad's on the verge of tears. He takes a quick picture of us before we leave.

Garrett is the perfect gentleman, opening my door for me. I love that approving look in his eyes.

"You look tasty in that dress, babe," he says to me once we're in his car. His tongue snakes out of his mouth in a quick motion.

"And you're looking mighty fine in that suit."

He bobs his head to the music as he drives away. I keep thinking about how good it's going to feel to have his arms wrapped around me.

Garrett is attentive to my every need at prom, from picture taking to pulling my chair out and making sure I ate before he did. It's the first time that Garrett and I have danced a real dance. I don't know what it is about tonight that feels different. With his arms holding me, I feel like he'll never let me go. When his lips brush against my skin, it's like silk. Every move he makes is calculated and leading up to a purpose.

Prom was everything I thought it would be, and it was over far too quickly. I wasn't ready for the night to end, and Garrett seemed to have the same idea.

"Do you want to take a ride with me?"

"Sure, where to?"

"You'll see."

That's Garrett's response to everything. I don't know why I bother to ask. He squeezes my hand slightly to reassure me. He surprises me by taking us to his favorite spot on the beach. He lays out the blanket that he pulled from the back seat and wraps another one around our shoulders. The wind blows easily. The temperature outside keeps it from being too cool.

"I wish this night didn't have to end," I say into the wind. I stare out into the ocean.

"It is a remarkable night. I can think of only one thing that would make it perfect."

Garrett turns me in his arms to face him. His eyes sparkle beneath the bright moon. I get lost in his gaze. I fall victim to his touch. He kisses me deeply, begging for more. As much as I want to go all the way, my conscious mind tells me that tonight is not the night.

I slow our kiss and our mouths part. "Garrett, I can't."

He looks at me, confused before his head dips in acceptance. "It's alright. I would never force you into anything you aren't ready for."

Disappointment is evident in his eyes. He pulls me close to him, and I lay my head on his shoulder. I can sense how bad he wants to continue. I felt the exact same way up until a few moments ago. All of the warnings and pep talks that I've received lately choose now to flash like a red flag. I'm not ready.

I stay curled up in Garrett's arms for a little while longer. Then he takes me home. It's a night I will remember for the rest of my life, and though Garrett didn't have his way, I feel like things couldn't have gone better.

Chapter 19

Bradley
One Year Earlier

Our final reports have been given for the year. Our lockers are cleared out, and Val and I came to the park to relax. While everyone else is planning to attend the end of school year parties, I have everything I want right next to me.

"Do you know where you're going?" I glance over at Val.

"Mom said we are going to stay with my aunt Kim in Ohio until she closes on the new house."

"Have you ever been there before?"

"Mom says that I have when I was younger. I don't remember going. My aunt is pretty cool, though. She's been here to visit us a few times."

"Are you excited about moving and starting over?"

Val thinks over my question. "I guess I am. The only downside to all of this is leaving you behind." She bumps her shoulder to mine. "What am I going to do without my playboy?" she says jokingly. The expression on her face turns serious. "I never told you what happened and why we need to leave."

"You don't have to Val. It's okay."

"No. I think I need to. I've never talked about it in depth with anyone, not even my mother. I've kept it bottled up for years. Maybe if I let it out, I can finally move on."

I grab hold of her hand to offer my support and nod for her to continue. I brace myself for what she's about to tell me. Whatever it is, it has to be disturbing enough for them to want to run from it.

"I was a normal kid once believe it or not. We were a typical family. I used to think we had a perfect life until I got old enough to start noticing the scars. My mom was really good at hiding them. She would always tell me that everything was fine. He didn't mean to do it. It was all her fault. I was naive enough to believe her. My dad had a bad temper, but he never showed it around me. He was always so careful not to hit her in front of me, until the one day he just didn't care. He was so angry with her that day, about dinner of all things. She tried to reason with him, saying that my practice ran late, but he wouldn't hear it. When he hit her, something snapped inside of me. Knowing that mom was being abused was one thing but actually seeing it…"

Val pauses and shakes her head as her eyes fall closed.

"I had to do something. I was only twelve years old, but I had to try. He beat me so bad that day that I ended up in the hospital, inches away from death. He ended up in jail for attempted murder and a few other charges. Mom has never forgiven herself for what happened to me. That house is a constant reminder of our past, a constant reminder of my coward dad and the father I will never have."

I pull Val into my chest, and she relaxes onto me. She blows out a long breath. I can feel the tension leaving her body. My heart aches for Val. That's a lot for anyone to have to carry. I wish I could take it all away for her.

***

Since school let out for the summer, Val and I have been spending every free moment we can together. This time tomorrow, she will be gone. Now I know the true meaning of that old saying, *time flies when you're having fun.*

I finally built up the courage to talk to her about her leaving. My family was surprised to hear the news. I think mom was even a little disappointed. They have all grown to love Val, just as I have.

Mom is having a cookout today for Val as a sort of a going-away celebration. I couldn't keep it a secret this time, and it will only be us; no additional family or friends. Maybe after the cookout, I can steal her away for a little while.

It's a beautiful sunny day outside. I tilt my head up to the sun, using my hand as a buffer. I couldn't have asked for a more perfect day for Val's celebration. Gin and Hale are inside making the salad. I can see dad at the grill, flipping burgers from the doorway. I step outside to help mom, who is hustling about making sure that everything is near perfect. I told her she didn't have to go to all of this trouble. Of course, she wouldn't listen. It's what makes her happy, and there is no changing her mind once it's made up.

I walk over to her at the picnic table set up in the backyard. She tears open the packaging from the table cover.

"Mom, let me help you with that."

We spread the cover and place the centerpiece.

"Is Valerie on her way over?"

"She should be here any minute now. She's bringing her mom. I hope that's okay."

"Why wouldn't it be? I would love to finally meet her. Is Val anything like her?"

"I've only seen her a hand full of times, but she seems to be."

Mom looks at me as if she can sense something inside of me. "How are you feeling, son? Have you come to grips with Valerie leaving?"

If she would've asked me that question one month ago or even a week ago, my answer would've been no. I didn't know how to process it at first. So, I tried to pretend that it wasn't happening. After Val and I talked, I felt much better about their decision to go. I understand why they need to leave now.

"I'll be okay. It's going to take some getting used to, not having Val around all of the time, but I'll be fine eventually.

Mom gives me a sympathetic look. "I can't believe I had it all wrong. I was sure the two of you..." She cuts her sentence short and smiles. Her hand pats my cheek softly. "I'm sorry you're losing your best friend, son."

I know exactly what mom wanted to say and didn't. It's what everyone thought. "It's probably for the best. It's the best thing for them, and I'm not losing her. We promised to keep in touch."

Someone my age should not have to deal with this type of stuff. I guess I should've expected something to come along and knock me off balance again. Things were going too well. I let myself get too comfortable with Val, but it's okay. It was great while it lasted.

"Well, there's that to look forward to," mom says in reply.

"Yeah, I guess so."

"Look who I found creeping around our front door," Gin announces.

Val and her mom follow her into the backyard. Her mom smiles, and Val grins.

"We were not creeping. I was just about to ring the doorbell when you swung the door open," Val says to Gin.

Since the two of them started their girl talks, they've become entertainingly close. I love to watch them bicker back and forth; my two best girls.

I walk over to Val and give her an awkward hug. I feel out of place, showing affection in front of her mother. I shake her mother's hand.

"Hi, Ms. Landon. This is my mom, Laura," I say, introducing our mothers.

Mom reaches out to shake Ms. Landon's hand. "Hi. It's nice to finally meet you."

"You too. Val talks about your family quite a bit."

Val turns away, embarrassed by her mom's statement. I smirk and squeeze her hand. I'm glad I'm not the only one who can't stop thinking about her and me.

I whisper in Val's ear. "Should we leave them to get acquainted?"

She nods, yes.

"We'll go bring out the supplies and let the grownups talk," I say to my mom with a wink.

"Good idea," she agrees. "Don't forget the cutlery."

I hear Ms. Landon complimenting mom on the decorations as we walk away with Gin on our tails. Gin pops me on my arm as she bypasses us just inside the back door. I feel outnumbered already with all of the females in the house.

"Is Jeremy coming over today?" I ask Gin.

"I think so."

"Good. This house could use some more testosterone today," I say teasingly.

"You're kidding yourself. Jeremy would never take your side over mine."

"You'll be surprised what a guy would do when they're backed into a corner, sis."

"Anyway… Aren't you supposed to be grabbing the cutlery? You best get to it hotshot."

"I'm going to miss both of you so much," Val says in between our bickering. We both turn to look at her and join in a group hug.

"We are going to miss you too. I know for sure that this knucklehead will," Gin says, glancing over to me.

"Gin, promise me you'll look after him for me. He's going to need someone to talk to, and I wouldn't necessarily recommend our friends. They may steer him in the wrong direction."

"Are you sure you want to leave him in my hands? I've been known to be a bit of an influence myself." Gin wiggles her brows playfully.

Val laughs. "Better you than them. Besides, it was always you before I ever dropped into the picture. I guess I should be thanking you for letting me borrow him." Val's look turns somber. "I wish I didn't have to give him back."

"You could always stuff him in a suitcase and take him with you." Gin tries to make light of the situation.

They're talking about me like I'm not standing right next to them. "Hello, have you two forgotten that I'm standing right here? Don't I get a say in all of this?"

Gin gives me a sly look. "Haven't you heard? Guys never know what they need. You should stay out of this. Let us handle it."

"Since you two are double-teaming me, I'm going to get Hale to help me carry the supplies out to mom."

I back away slowly and turn to get Hale. She's sitting on the couch reading a book. I smile as I approach her. She doesn't even look up. Whenever she's reading, it's like nothing around her exists.

"Hey, Hale. What are you reading?"

She looks up at me with wide eyes. I can tell she's annoyed with my interruption. "Harry Potter," she says bluntly.

I want to ask her why she's reading that again, but I know better. I tilt my head to one side, silently asking her the question.

"I know what you're thinking, and it's only my second time reading it. I've already come across a detail that I had missed the first time. You should give the books a try. They are really good."

I respectfully decline. "Maybe someday, I will. Right now, I have to take some things out to mom. Would you like to help me?"

Hale glances over at Val and Gin, then back to me. They're in the kitchen engaged in conversation. Hale's look asks, why me?

"Come on, Hale. We're about to get started. It will be fun. You can even invite Amy over. She's right up the street. It shouldn't take her long to get here."

She perks up at the mention of her best friend coming over. "Okay. I will help you, and then I'll call Amy."

We take the supplies outside to mom. Dad finishes up with the food. I'm glad to see Hale in a better mood when Amy arrives. I wish there weren't a disconnect between us. It's inevitable with our age difference, though.

Mom, dad, and Ms. Landon are getting along really well, and I wonder why it took them leaving for my and Val's parents to meet. It could've always been like this, with us sitting around talking, eating, laughing.

The day goes by too quickly, and before I know it, Val's mom is ready to leave. She lets Val stay behind since it's her last night here. I promise to bring her home later.

Val and I lay beneath the stars in my backyard, looking up at the moon. Our hands are joined between us. Our time together is quickly coming to an end. We're both quiet. Neither one of us knows the correct thing to say right now.

Val's voice breaks through my thoughts. "So, tomorrow?" she whispers.

"So, tomorrow," I say in response.

"How do we do this, Brad? I didn't expect it to be this hard."

I turn to face her. My mind mimics her thoughts. *How do we do this?* "This isn't the end, Val. We'll still talk all the time. I'm just a phone call away." That's the way I'm hoping it will be, but even I know distance is a problem. People grow apart.

"I love you, Brad. I will never forget you."

"I love you too, Val." I pull her close to me when her tears begin to fall. I kiss her softly and meaningfully.

I have so many selfish questions streaming through my mind. Will she be happy without me? How do I move on from the past two years of my life? The most important question at the forefront; how do I say goodbye to my best distraction?

Chapter 20

Samantha

One Year Earlier

I've been so busy lately with swimming that I hardly have time to spend with Garrett anymore. It's been a constant loop of school, practice, home, and repeat. I only see him in school during the day and sometimes on Saturday, but it's not the same. I miss him. I feel like we're drifting apart. I've expressed my concerns with him. Of course, he says that we are fine. I just have to get through two more weeks of school. Then maybe we can spend more time together.

Garrett wasn't in our last class. I wonder where he was as I put my things away. I hear him coming down the hall before I see him. The sound of his voice always brings a smile to my face. Just as I close my locker, he swings me around and dips me.

"Hey, babe. I missed you." His grip loosens around my back, and his hands rest on my waist.

"I missed you too."

"It's my favorite part of the day."

"Yeah, I know. It's lunchtime. Unfortunately, I have to go to the library during my break. So, I have to eat fast."

"We better get going then." He throws his arm around my shoulder and guides me down the hall.

"Why weren't you in class today?" I ask hesitantly.

"Coach excused us all from class for a special meeting about next season."

I can't help but notice the funny looks as we walk. The popular girls giggle and whisper as we pass. It's like everyone knows a secret that I don't. I glance at Garrett to see if it's just me or if he notices too.

"Are you alright, babe?"

"Am I missing something? Do you feel everyone's eyes on us, or is it just me?"

"It's just you," he answers quickly. "These people could care less what we do. You're just paranoid. How are things with the swim team?" He changes the subject.

I still feel uneasy about the stares, but I'll let it go for now. "Things are good. Are you coming to my swim meet on Saturday? You haven't made it to one yet."

"You know I have to work, babe. I wish I could be there."

Garrett has been working a lot lately. His workdays seem to always fall on the same days as my swim meets. He hasn't been much support in that area. Dad and Lacy have been to all of them. Most days, when I have practice, Garrett is off from work. Our schedules are on opposite sides of the spectrum.

"I understand. I wish you could come check out my moves. I'm like a mermaid when I'm in the water."

"You do know that the water is not the only place you can show me your moves, right?" he asks jokingly.

I swat his arm playfully. "Leave it to you to corrupt something innocent. That mouth of yours is going to get you in trouble one day."

We grab our trays and find a seat. Garrett leans over to whisper in my ear. The warmth from his breath stimulates my inner ear.

"If I'm able to corrupt it, it wasn't innocent in the first place, babe."

I cough at his statement, trying not to choke. I have a feeling he wasn't talking about swimming. My appetite for food is long gone. I eat the veggies and stand to leave, just as everyone else takes a seat. As I walk away, I hear Garrett laughing behind me. The last two people I want to see just walked into the cafeteria, Cindy and Michelle. I try to pretend that I don't see them. They have hated me since the moment they found out about Garrett and me. With all of the unwanted attention that I've gotten today from everyone else, I don't want to add them to the list. To avoid their ugly stares, I keep my eyes forward. I hear Michelle giggling at something Cindy is saying. As I pass them, they speak to me in unison.

"Hi, Samantha."

I ignore them and keep walking. Why did they pick today of all days to mess with my head? I want to stop and ask them what is going on, but that could lead to a brawl. They're not worth my time or energy.

I check out the book I need from the library. On the way to my next class, Cindy passes me in the hallway smiling widely. Just past her, I see Garrett leaning against his locker, watching her walk away. When he sees me, his stance changes. I stop directly in front of him. I can't tell if the smile on his face is real or just for show.

Did I see what I think I did?

Is my mind playing tricks on me?

I shake my head to clear the demons lurking about. "Hey."

Garrett grabs my waist and gazes into my eyes. "Hey, babe."

"What was that about?" I ask him, throwing my thumb in the direction Cindy just went.

"What was what about?" He scrunches his brows in confusion.

Maybe it was all in my mind. Maybe all of the stares and whispers are starting to get to me, and I'm seeing things that aren't really happening. "Nothing, I just thought... it's nothing." I decided against bringing it up. He obviously doesn't know what I'm talking about. It already feels like we're falling apart without throwing my insecurities into the mix.

Garrett walks me to my next class. I'm content today being away from him for a few more hours. I'm going to surprise him today. He doesn't know it yet, but I don't have practice. He doesn't have to work. So, we can finally spend some much-needed time together outside of school.

When school lets out, instead of going to practice, I linger around until I see Garrett walking towards his car. He looks serious and walks with purpose like he's on a mission. I wonder what his plans are for this evening? What does he do when he's not working and not with me?

Just as I make a move to find out, I see Cindy run up to him. She weaves her arm through his and smiles up at him. He startles at first until recognition hits him. He returns her smile and makes no move to untangle himself from her arm. I'm more confused now than ever. My mind says go to him, but I can't seem to move my feet. So, I stand there and watch it play out.

Cindy let's go of his arm and splits away from him. They're still talking, but at least they aren't so close. I finally blink and breathe a sigh of relief when she goes in the opposite direction. My solace is short-lived. The moment Cindy jumps in the passenger seat of Garrett's car, my breathing stills. When Garrett gets in and leans over to kiss her, my heart breaks. I see them drive away together, but still, I can't move.

It's hard to process what I've just witnessed. It's hard to describe what I'm feeling right now. There has to be some explanation. I think back over the past week in school, all of the sideways glances, the whispers, and giggles. Does this have something to do with it? Why would he lie to me? How could he do this to me? Then, it dawns on me. Everyone knew about them… everyone but me. He made me the laughing stock of the entire school. How can I ever show my face here again?

When the fog begins to disappear, the voices become clearer, and the laughter even louder. Students have noticed me standing here with my heart torn out, and no one comes to comfort me. I should never have distanced myself from everyone else because of him. His friends, everyone that we hung out with from time to time, are not my friends. They all knew and didn't say one word.

The words come to me freely now.

Pained.

Broken.

Betrayed.

Done.

I decide that I'm done with Garrett Wright, but something inside of me still wants to know why.

I had planned on riding home with Garrett today. So, I asked dad to drop me off this morning on his way to work. *Look how well that turned out*, I think to myself. Lacy gets off early on Friday. I know she will come to get me if I asked, but I'm too embarrassed to call her. She warned me about Garrett, and I didn't listen. I can't bear to face her right now, so I start walking. It will be good for me and give me a chance to either clear my mind or think it through.

When I get home, I'm tired from walking and thinking. I just want to be by myself tonight. It's not even five o'clock yet, but I can't bring myself to do anything else. I wash up, jump into bed, and cry myself to sleep.

***

I have my swim meet today. I still haven't figured out what to do about Garrett. I've been ignoring his calls since I found out about him and Cindy. I wonder if he even knows that I busted him. I know that I will eventually have to talk to him. Right now, I need to concentrate on the competition today. My placement today will determine if I move on to the next round or not.

I smile at dad and Lacy up in the stands. Dad blows out a loud whistle, and Lacy waves frantically. I make sure that my cap is secure on my head, and my goggles are snug over my eyes. Today I'm swimming the one-hundred-meter breaststroke. Coach Farley usually has me swim last in case I need to pick up the slack if someone were to fall behind for some reason. I used to feel pressured by that choice, but now it doesn't bother me one bit.

Coach Farley comes up to me to offer words of encouragement. I nod as I take in her words. I shake my limbs loose and blow out a long breath. The noise around me fades away, and I dive in when I hear the pop. Once my body hits the water, we become one. I don't think about anything else. The room temperature water cascades across my skin as I move. I feel like I'm outside of my body. I pace my breathing to match my movements. When my final lap is over, and I come up for air, and the cheers creep in slowly. Whether I win or not, this is always the best part, knowing that I've finished it, and there are people out there rooting for me.

I walk back to my teammates. I hear a congratulatory scream in the crowd with my name attached to it and turn to look into the crowd for dad and Lacy. Garrett is standing beside Lacy, shouting my name. One moment I'm in the clouds, and in the next, I'm thrown back into yesterday in the school parking lot. I wasn't expecting to see him here today. He told me he had to work. Was that a lie too? I give dad and Lacy a wave and quickly turn away. How dare he show up here after shattering my heart to pieces?

I placed second overall in the meet today. So, I'm moving on to the next round. That piece of good news is the only thing keeping me from smacking Garrett when I walk up to my family.

Dad pulls me in for a hug. "You did great, Sammy. I'm so proud of you."

Lacy throws her arms around me. "You deserve first place after that performance."

"Thank you both. I'm just glad I made the cut at all." I cut my eyes at Garrett.

"Congratulations, babe," he says to me like nothing ever happened.

I stay quiet. Now is not the time to cause a scene. Garrett reaches for my hand, and I let him take it to keep up appearances. I need to tell dad and Lacy, but not here.

He looks at my dad and asks the one question I was hoping he wouldn't. "Mr. Young, would you mind if I drove Samantha home?"

Dad looks at me, searching my face for any objection. I wonder if the show that I'm putting on is working. Can he sense my pain?

"If that's what Sammy wants to do, I'm okay with it."

"Just have her home at a decent hour," Lacy says jokingly.

"I'm kind of tired anyway. We'll be right behind you," I say. I purposefully look into Garrett's eyes, letting him know that the car ride home is all the time he has to say what he needs to say.

Lacy studies me and nods. She must sense that something is wrong. "Okay, I'll see you at home."

She hardly ever comes straight over after one of my swim meets. Now I feel bad for not telling her. I kept it to myself because I know what she will say. No one likes to be told, '*I told you so*.'

Dad and Lacy drive ahead, and I reluctantly get into the passenger seat of Garrett's car. The very same seat that Cindy was in when he kissed her. I wonder what else he and Cindy have done in this car. My body is tense from trying not to touch anything. It just doesn't feel the same, being here with Garrett. Our memory is tainted.

He puts the car in gear and drives away. I look straight ahead, waiting for him to tell me what I already know. I fear that if I look at him, he will somehow make my pain disappear, and I'll fall right back into him.

I listen as his breath starts and stops over and over again, trying to form words that won't make a difference after the car ride. "Samantha," he finally manages to get out. "I don't know what to say. It didn't mean anything. She doesn't mean anything to me. I've only been with her a few times."

My blood is boiling. I didn't know it was possible for a heart to feel a continuous break. I don't know what I expected. Maybe I was hoping that he would lie to me and tell me that nothing had happened, that I imagined things.

"Then why, Garrett? How could you do this to me?" I finally turn to look at him. The pull that I thought would be there is replaced by a mountain of hurt.

"I'm so sorry, babe. I Love you. I promise it will never happen again," comes his weak attempt at redemption.

"No, Garrett. You're not sorry, and you don't love me. If you did, we wouldn't be having this conversation right now. How long has it been going on?"

"Babe..."

"You know what, it doesn't matter. I asked you, Garrett, and you lied to me. You let me think that I was paranoid. You had everyone laughing at me to my face, and you knew why."

Garrett pulls into my driveway and puts the car into park.

"Babe, please. You have to understand. You are always busy. We hardly spend any time together anymore. She was just…"

"Stop it, Garrett. You don't get to call me babe anymore, and don't try to make this my fault. I won't let you do that to me. You are right about one thing. It will never happen again, not to me. From now on, you are free to do whatever and with whomever you want. This…" I motion between the two of us. "This is over, and it's all because of you. The next time you see me, do me the courtesy of forgetting who I am."

I get out and slam the door. I don't look back before I enter my home. Lacy is waiting there for me with open arms, just like I knew she would be. We sit down on the couch, and for the first time all day, I let the tears fall. She lets me cry on her shoulder without knowing the cause. I imagine if mom were here, she would do the same. I imagine that she would be proud of me for staying strong and standing up for myself.

Chapter 21

Bradley

Present Day

The past year has been tough. When Val left, I had so much time on my hands. We talked every day for a few weeks. As she settled into her new life, our calls turned into texts, and over time our texts became less frequent. I miss her, but I'm happy for her and her mom. They're finally free from all of the memories.

I fell back into my old routine. My books have been my refuge these days. My main focus is college right now. I'm still on track to do all that I set out to do.

Graduation is a huge deal in our house this year. I sympathize with my parents having two at the same time. The preparation for graduation is even more of a headache than prom. There is so much more that I'm required to do. There is no way of getting around it unless I don't want to walk across the stage on graduation day. So, I suck it up and roll with the flow. My mom won't let me skip out anyway since I'm the class valedictorian. I'm supposed to give a speech at the ceremony, and I have no idea what I'm going to say. Gin volunteered to help me with it. I don't know if her words will be adult appropriate, but I agreed to let her help. If we come up with the speech together, I can have Gin up there with me, though not physically.

"We have to finish this tonight, BP. Why don't we try saying something like *all of us have traveled a long road together, and we have made it to the finish line? Whatever comes next is up to us to decide. For some of us, that may be scary to think of, but keep in mind the words and actions of those that came before us. We are all more than capable of anything. We can all have what our minds desire. Find what it is that captures your heart, reach for it, and it can be yours."*

I look at my sister, proud of who she has become. Gin actually has some great ideas for the speech. I'm intrigued by her attention and determination to get this done. I was disappointed when she announced to the family that she was not going to a traditional college, though it didn't surprise me. Gin has always been a free spirit. I always knew that she would find some way to spruce up her educational experience. She will be going away to culinary school soon, while I attend the local college. This will be the first time that we've ever been apart for a long period of time.

"I should just let you write the entire speech," I say to Gin.

"You would like that, wouldn't you?"

"I didn't think you would be this interested in writing a speech. I think this is your calling. You should be a professional speechwriter."

Gin whacks me across my shoulder with the notepad. "That is the last thing that I want. It would drive me nuts, the deadlines, the meetings, the constant need to come up with something new. That's just not me. I want to make people happy through food. I want to travel, climb a few mountains, go bungee jumping… I'm not meant to be stuck in one place, no offense."

"None taken, sis. I can see that those things will make you happy. You light up when you talk about it. I feel the same way about the direction I'm headed."

"Where do you think you'll be this time next year?" Gin places the notepad onto the table and slouches down on the couch, kicking her feet up on the ottoman.

I mimic her movements. "I don't know. Maybe I'll be married with a kid on the way, living in an apartment and working nights just to make ends meet."

"That's very specific. It's almost believable. You should take up acting."

I laugh at Gin's comment. "Seriously, though, I was thinking about doubling up on classes and even taking summer courses to finish early. I could probably be done in two and a half years if I push myself."

She looks at me, skeptically. "What's the rush? Don't you want to have time for other things? Like living life, for example? Wouldn't you like to fall in love one day? When will you have time to do that if you're always hitting the books?"

I don't know if I should tell Gin about my life plan or not. She will probably think I'm insane. I never want to fall in love, not completely. "There will be plenty of time, when I'm done with school," I respond half truthful. "What about you? Do you think that Jeremy is the one?"

Her expression softens when I mention Jeremy. "I love Jeremy. I hope that we will still be together one year from now, but I'm not a fool, BP. Things can change in the blink of an eye. Jeremy and I are from different sides of the same coin. Sure, today, we mix well together. There's nothing in the rulebook that says it will remain that way. I've heard that the first two years after high school is the most difficult. I think if we can withstand that period of time, we'll be okay. We both have a lot to figure out and a lot more growing up to do."

I nod my head in approval. "I like the way you think."

"So do I," Gin says playfully. "And if things don't work out between us, I'll manage. Any guy would be lucky to have me."

"You're absolutely right. Don't ever change, Gin."

***

My alarm clock screams at me to get up and going. I hit the snooze button and pull the covers over my head. I grumble at the loud knocking on my door a few minutes later.

"BP! Rise and shine. Today is the first day of the rest of your life." Gin shouts loudly in the hallway.

I can hear her giggling on the other side of the door. I'm about to protest until realization dawns on me. There was a reason I set the alarm earlier this morning. It's graduation day. I sit upright in the bed, still not wanting to start the day but knowing that I have to.

"I'm up! I'm up!" I shout back to her. This is not how I want to spend my Saturday.

"You have thirty minutes, and I'm coming in." I hear Gin's footsteps tapping down the hall away from my door.

Mom had insisted that we all get up in time this morning. She wants us to sit around the table and have a family breakfast. *"It will be our last one for a long time,"* she said. I think she's hiding her feelings about both Gin and me leaving home at the same time. I have to keep reminding her that I'm not going anywhere. I'll only be a few miles away.

I want to have the full college experience, even though I'm staying in the city. I will be moving into the dorms. I want to be where all of the action is, and I won't have to worry about mom peeping over my shoulders every day. It won't stop her from calling, but it's better that way.

I climb out of bed and hop into the shower. I take an extra thirty minutes getting ready, just to see if Gin would make good on her threat. I put on some shorts and a t-shirt for now, in case breakfast gets messy.

Gin is standing beside my open room door when I step out of my bathroom. Her arms are folded across her chest as she glares at me, trying to hold a straight face.

"What?" I ask her with a soft chuckle.

A burst of laughter springs from her. "You know *what*," she emphasizes. "You did that on purpose, didn't you?"

"Did what? I got up. I got dressed."

"Okay, smart-aleck. Breakfast is ready, and you've already wasted precious time and water with your over-the-top shower."

I'm going to miss our playful bickering. I think to myself as we make our way into the dining room. Everyone is seated already. Mom gives me a reprimanding look, and I avert my eyes to avoid her stare. Dad is smiling at mom's expression, and Hale is sitting next to him, grinning softly. My disregard for Gin's earlier warning has gotten me in trouble.

"Sorry, mom. I didn't realize that you were all waiting for me." I squint my eyes at Gin as I sit. She knew this would happen and didn't warn me. She covers her laughter with her hands.

Dad clears his throat to speak. "Two of our babies are finally leaving the nest, Laura," he says to mom.

"I know. It seems like it was just yesterday when they were lying in my arms, needing me to do everything for them."

"That *was* yesterday," Gin says.

"You know what I mean, Ginger," mom says. "You were just babies, and now you're all grown up and ready to embark on the great adventure."

"When are you leaving, GG?" Dad asks Gin.

School doesn't start for her until fall. She and Jeremy are going ahead to find a place to stay.

"Next weekend… Our flight is supposed to leave around ten Saturday morning," Gin answers.

"Do you know where you're going to stay yet?" dad asks.

"Mom helped us find a nice hotel until we settle on a place. The search should be interesting, considering neither of us knows the place that well. The school said they could send someone to help us if we needed it." Gin pops a grape into her mouth. I can tell she doesn't really want to talk about leaving.

"Are you sure you don't want your dad and me to come with you, just for a week or two? I can take some time off, and I'm sure your dad has some personal time saved up," mom asserts.

"Mom, we've talked about this. I think it's best if we go alone. I need to figure things out for myself," Gin replies.

"Bradley, you'll be sticking around for a few more months. How do you feel about helping me out at work this summer?"

Dad looks at me, hesitantly. I'm surprised by his question. We barely talk in passing. I guess he feels like this would be a good way to change things. I've spent years trying not to know him. Maybe it's time that I try.

"Sounds great," I say with false happiness. Maybe if I hype myself up, it will be a lot easier when it happens.

Mom smiles wide at the both of us. I think she's been hoping for this moment for a long time, but she would never say it out loud.

"Can we eat breakfast now?" Hale says what I have been thinking since I walked into the room. Everyone breaks into laughter.

After breakfast, Gin and I get dressed and drive over to the school for one last run-through of the ceremony before it begins. Excitement reverberates throughout the air. Everyone wants to know what's next. What school are you going to? Do they look okay? Are their cap and gown on correctly? Is anyone having a graduation party? So many questions.

The only thing I'm concerned with is getting through my speech and taking my final walk across the stage.

One of the senior instructors comes in and announces that it's time to line up. I'm the first in line and the first to see all of the families anxiously waiting for a familiar face that they know to emerge. I'm nervous, but I don't let it show. I keep my head high and walk proudly to the stage, while my classmates sit in the chairs just below facing us. It hadn't really hit me until now what an honor this truly is.

When it's my turn to speak, I step up to the microphone, and the words pour out like I had been practicing for months. I'll have to tell Gin thanks again for helping me. I received a couple of laughs, and I saw a few tears in the crowd too. It feels good knowing that these words may someday be remembered and make a difference to someone out there.

"Bradley Pierce." They call my name, and I walk up to receive my diploma with a beaming smile.

It's time for us to begin the next phase of our lives. Every decision that we make from now on will have adult consequences. After this past year, I'm more than ready.

Chapter 22

Samantha

Present Day

I haven't spoken to Garrett since our breakup last year. He has tried to reach out to me plenty since then. I can't bear to put myself through that kind of hurt again. After a few weeks, I took action and blocked his phone number. I tried my best not to bypass him in the hallway at school. He finally gave up trying and reverted back to his old ways. The leeches are back in full effect, just like before.

Lacy has been a Godsend through all of this. For weeks, she watched my self-loathing and listened to my cries. She lent me her shoulder and held my hand when I needed it to be held. Not once did she judge me for my actions. Dad has been there for me as well. He doesn't speak about what happened. He has, however, cheered me up on more than one occasion. He is always trying to find something to try and keep my mind off of Garrett. He and Lacy are my greatest comforts. They lifted me up when I felt like I was at my lowest point.

I have thought a lot about my relationship with Garrett. For a long time, I blamed myself for his wrongdoing. I kept wondering if it was something that I did to cause him to turn to someone else. I asked myself question after question. Was I not pretty enough? Would things be different if I had given in to him that night after prom? Should I have spent less time and energy on swimming and more time with him? What is it about her that made him risk what he had with me? So many questions…

The more I thought about it, the more I began to realize that those questions held no merit. I started on a mission to recovery. Every day that passed, I would tell myself that I was not the problem. I'm beautiful, smart, and Garrett didn't deserve me. His mom was right. Her son is not ready for a girl like me. He has a lot of growing up to do.

I put all of my being into loving Garrett, and in the end, I was taught a valuable lesson. Love played a game with my heart, and I lost. In my defeat, I've learned that I shouldn't be so trusting. Boys are nothing but trouble. I've been taught that a wall is the only thing standing in the way of my mended heart and the next disaster. I am positive that there is no one tall enough to climb it or strong enough to knock down the barrier that I've built.

Today is one of the most important days of my life, and I'm sitting here reminiscing about Garrett. I know I will see him today, probably with Cindy or Michelle. I remind myself that after today, I never have to see him and his leeches ever again. I shake my head of thoughts about him. I should be focusing on making it to the school on time. I stand up from the desk in my bedroom and walk over to the bed to make sure that everything is in order, one last time.

Black slacks, white shirt, black flats, cap, and gown… check. My nerves are on edge. This is the third time this morning that I've clicked off this list in my head.

"Sammy," my dad calls from outside my door.

"Yes, dad?" He is just as excited about today as I am. I smile to myself, imagining dad tapping his feet against the floor. It's seventy-one degrees in here, and he's probably sweating like crazy.

"What time are you supposed to be at the school again?"

I have told him this more than once over the past few days, and every time he says, *I'm just making sure. I don't want you to miss it.*

"I have to be there in an hour. I was just about to get dressed."

"When you're ready, I'll be in the living room."

"Okay, dad."

I get dressed quickly and slip my shoes on. Moments later, there's a knock at the door. Lacy enters without an answer and closes the door behind her.

"Lacy, you made it!" I run over and give her a huge hug.

"Of course, I did, Grace. I wouldn't miss this for anything in the world. My baby sister is graduating. It's hard to believe." She places her palm against my cheek and tilts her head to the side in silent thought. A sliver of breath oozes from her mouth. "Is there anything I can help you with?"

"I think I'm all set." My eyes roam the room.

"Before we go, I want to say something. Can we sit for a minute?"

"Sure." We sit on the edge of my bed, and Lacy takes my hand in hers.

"I am so proud of you, Grace. You've come a long way from the baby I used to hold all of those years ago. I feel like mom would have made some big speech, and God only knows what she would say."

Lacy chuckles slightly and tilts her head up to the ceiling for a few seconds. I sometimes forget that we've missed out on some of the same things. Sure, she had mom for a little while, but she has never had the chance to share this day with mom either.

"Before you go out there in the world, I want to make sure you know your worth. You are smart, beautiful, strong, brave, talented, and so much more Grace. I know it, and dad knows it, but *you* have to believe it."

Lacy pauses, and I can see the wells forming in her eyes through the cloud in my own. She knows me better than anyone, and she believed in me when I couldn't do it for myself.

"You've gone through a rough patch, but don't let that one mishap keep you from something great. What you have gone through was horrible, and I'm sorry that it happened but know that there is life after Garrett. I want you to promise me that you won't close yourself off. If love finds you, don't push it away."

I know my worth, but I can't make that promise without telling a lie. Lacy seems to understand when I don't answer.

"I, at least, want you to try Grace," she pleads.

"I can try," I say with little confidence.

Lacy nods her head and gives me a hug. "Okay. Let's go and claim what you've worked all of these years for."

I could never hide anything from Lacy. I told her I would try, and I will, but my main focus is finishing college. I'm not looking for anything else, and if love finds me, my wall will be anything but easy to tear down.

***

Just as I expected, Garrett is surrounded when I pretend not to see him. I have managed to make a few friends since our split. Surprisingly, everyone at school is not Team Wright. My family is already here. They came along with me and had to wait outside until they opened the doors to let people in. I told dad I could drive, but he wasn't having it. I can still hear his voice earlier, saying, *"It's better to be on time than late."*

"Samantha!" My friend shouts my name over the crowd between us.

I spin around to face Kerri, who's rushing towards me. "Hey!" I throw my arms around her neck.

Kerri befriended me when I was at a very low point. There were days when I went to school, but my mind wasn't really there. I spent most of my time just going through the motions, sitting alone at lunch, and staring off into oblivion. Kerri was one of the ones that noticed. She came up to me one day while I was sitting under a tree outside the school. She said I looked like I could use a friend. She had wanted to do it for a while but always thought that I was unapproachable. There was something about me that day that compelled her to do it. She introduced me to her friends, Mags and Lenny, and they quickly became my friends too.

Before meeting them, I hadn't realized that people thought of me that way. It was laughable to me. All of these years, I thought I had a welcoming personality. I guess it depended on the people I surrounded myself with; cause and effect. Because I was with Garrett and his friends, I appeared to be just like them when that wasn't the case.

"Can you believe we're about to be free of this wormhole?"

I snicker at her comment. Kerri's sense of humor always brings me joy. "Wormhole?"

"Yeah, this place has been trying to suck me in since the first day."

"Well, I'm just glad the day is finally here. Have you given any more thought to coming to Ohma with me? We could be roommates," I say to try and convince her to come to college with me. I keep asking, and every time she finds a different way to tell me no.

I want to learn everything there is to know about food, and I want to learn from the best. So, I'm going to The Victual Institute in Ohma, PA for two years. From there, I will be going to Lakin University in Lakin, PA to take business courses.

Kerri shakes her head no. "I wouldn't make it there. I'm not made for that life. I'm going to stay right here in Hinton, where everything is familiar."

"Are you sure that a certain guy named Leonard doesn't factor into your decision?" I ask her.

She and Lenny have an on and off relationship. They can't decide if they want to be together or not. They have always remained friends, though. It gets really confusing. Right now, they are in 'on' status.

"No. What makes you say that?"

"Well, for starters, he's not going anywhere either." I raise my brows in question.

"That's just a coincidence."

"Whatever you say…" I trail off when I see Lenny and Mags approaching.

"What's up, guys?" Mags says excitedly.

Mags has a quirky personality. She reminds me of Blossom from that old show. Lenny is all serious and unreadable. He doesn't talk a lot, but when he does, people listen. He's also kind of cute. I can see why Kerri is smitten with him.

Lenny wraps one arm around Kerri's waist and says hi to us.

"I was trying to convince Kerri to tag along with me to school."

Mags huffs out a breath. "Good luck with that."

I don't miss that Lenny's hold on Kerri gets a little bit tighter. I smile at his reaction. I don't know why they refuse to admit that they don't want to be apart from each other.

"Graduates, may I have your attention?" Keith, our senior class president, voices over all of the noise.

We all quiet down and turn in his direction.

"We are about to begin shortly. I want to make sure that we are all in accord. We will line up by last name and be divided into two groups, one on the left and one on the right. If you need help with securing your hats or ties, now is the time to ask. Tassels should be worn on the right side of your caps. Any questions?" He pauses for responses, but no one does. "Okay, great. Everyone fall in line, just like we practiced. Let's get moving, and if I don't get to talk to any of you later, congratulations, everyone."

I turn back to my friends who have helped me out of my slump. "I guess it's that time, guys!"

They all nod their heads in agreement. We exchange hugs and move to our assigned spots.

A few moments later, we are walking out to be seated. The fact that I'm four spots behind Garrett in the line doesn't phase me at all. There is nothing that could dampen my mood today. I'm so wrapped up in excitement that I barely hear a word that's spoken until the names are being called.

I wait anxiously for my name and step into action when I hear it. It's my proudest moment, holding my diploma in my hands. The reality of my future really hits me when I turn to face the crowd and turn my tassel. I spot the approving faces of dad and Lacy in the audience. I grant them a quick wave and exit left stage. I'm ready for whatever comes next.

Part Two

When Love Finds You

Bradley & Samantha

Present Day

Chapter 23

Bradley

My first two years of college were not what I had expected. My outlook on relationships has changed since high school.

The summer after I graduated, I went to work with my dad. It was very awkward at first. I still harbored resentment towards him for things that happened in the past. I didn't know what to say to him or even how to begin a conversation. The crazy thing is when you work with someone, it's almost impossible not to speak, especially if you don't know what you're doing.

I was forced to ask questions about work, and before I knew it, we were taking lunch breaks together. Then he began to ask questions about me. It started with small stuff like sports and moved on to other things like school and what I wanted to do with the rest of my life. I answered every question honestly, but I couldn't get past my issues with him. There was something that I wanted to know after all of these years. I distinctly remember the conversation we had that summer.

"Dad, can I ask you a question, man to man?"

Dad takes a bite of his sandwich. He looks at me, amused by my choice of words. His head dips once, inviting me to continue. I should be nervous about the direction this is going in, but I'm not. I'm calm, and I've never felt more sure about something. It's time that I know his side of the story, even if I don't like what he has to say.

"The night that you got drunk and left us, what happened? One minute we were picking mom up, and the next you were gone. I never understood why." I stare at him, waiting for a response.

Dad looks away, seemingly pained by the memory. He clears his throat and turns back to look me straight in my eyes. "I always wondered when this day would come. There were so many times when I wanted to tell you about that day. I knew you blamed me for what happened. I always figured it would be easier if you believed everything was my fault."

I tilt my head slightly in wonder. What does he mean? It was all his fault.

"Do you remember us picking your mother up that evening?"

"Yes. I remember that. Mom was so happy that day." I smile at the memory.

"Then you remember the guy that she was with?" he asks me.

"Yes."

"I need to explain something before I get into why I did what I did. Your mom and I were happy in the beginning. We were inseparable. Over time we began to drift apart. It's no excuse, but we stopped making time for each other." He pauses for a moment. *"Let me rephrase that. I stopped making time for her. We were going through a rough patch financially. I was always working, and I put our personal needs on the back burner. I didn't notice what was going on until it was too late. I had my suspicions, but until the day I saw it with my own eyes, it didn't register. I would never have thought that she would turn to someone else."* He shakes his head in disbelief.

I'm stunned at what I'm hearing. What is he trying to say? "Mom cheated on you?"

Dad smirks sadly. "I guess that would depend on your definition of cheating. She wasn't physically involved with the guy but emotionally, yes. Finding that out hurt me just as bad as if she had committed the act. If I hadn't seen them together that day, who knows where things would have led. When I confronted her about it that night, she told me that she loved him. She told me she was sorry. She told me that she would never see him again. I couldn't wrap my head around that at that moment. I needed time to think. That's why I left. If I had stayed in the state that I was in, I don't know what I would've done."

I hang my head in shame. All of this time I've wasted trying not to love my dad, keeping my distance. I've avoided him and treated him like a stranger. "So, you left."

"Yes, I did. That was probably one of the best decisions that I've ever made. My leaving forced us both to step back and reflect on what the cause of our problem was. It was nothing against you kids. I would never abandon you. I just had to give myself time to either accept and deal with the situation or learn to walk away. It took me some time, but I've come to terms with what your mother did. I've accepted my part in all of this too. I'm not excusing her behavior, but I forgive her. I love her, and that's the only way that we could move on. My family is important to me. If I didn't try, I would never forgive myself."

"I'm sorry, dad, for the way that I've treated you throughout the years. If I had known..."

Dad cuts me off with a wave of his hand. "And that's exactly why I didn't say anything. You were young, and you needed your mother. I couldn't have you resenting her for something we were both responsible for. I figured I was the better choice."

That conversation changed my whole perspective on everything. I finally have both sides to the story, and now that I know, I can't say that I blame either of them. It was just one of those things that happened. Sure, it made me see my mom in a different light, but I don't love her any less. It's in the past. They have moved on from it. Who am I to judge? My dad and I still aren't where we should be, mostly because of my guilt, but we're working on it.

I've made some new friends and gone on a few dates since our talk but nothing came of them. I guess it's hard to break old habits. As open as I try to be, I haven't met anyone who awakens my senses, and I'm not one hundred percent sure that I want to risk my heart.

The plan that I made all those years ago still stands. I managed to cram three years of classes into two and still have somewhat of a social life. A few more courses and I will be done. I think I'll take it easy this year and let it play out gradually. I need to come up for air and enjoy this last year.

One thing that I will not miss about college is the dorms. My roommate, Nathan, and I get along great, but I can't wait to have my own space.

Nathan is on the football team along with our other friends, Philip and Garrett. I don't know how I got paired up with a jock for a roommate. It's pretty cool, I guess. I get first dibs on tickets to the games, and I'm always invited to their *extracurricular* activities. They made me an honorary member of the team, even though I don't play. The coach lets me practice with the team when I want. He has tried to recruit me on numerous occasions, to which I respectfully decline each time. I like the game, and practice is a good workout. I just don't see the point in committing myself to something that I'm not passionate about.

"Ugh," I grunt as the football barrels into my abdomen. I fall to the field in a sideways roll with the ball tucked neatly into the crease of my elbows.

"You alright, man?" Garrett comes over to give me a hand up. He is one of the toughest players on the team. Practicing alongside him has definitely made me stronger. I would hate to go up against him in an actual game.

I glare at him. Garrett is one of those guys that loves to brag without saying the words. It's one of the first things that I noticed about him.

"I'm fine," I say as I swat away his hand and stand up.

"I guess I don't know my own strength." He chuckles, and I want to punch him.

The way we behave on the field, you would never guess that we are good friends. He's actually a likable guy once you get past the ego. We are both extremely competitive on the field, but we never let that carry over into our daily lives.

A whistle sounds. "Wright… Pierce… move your asses." Coach Whale's voice booms across the field, and we both jump into action.

We go through a few more plays with Garrett and me behaving badly. When practice is over, we all spill into the locker room to freshen up. I'm gathering my things when I feel the sting across my back.

"Hey, Brad. Philip, Garrett and I are going to a party tonight. Are you down?" Nathan asks.

Partying with these three can get out of hand sometimes. Knowing that I hardly ever say no. They probably wouldn't let me if I tried. I'm always the designated driver. I pretend to think about it. I don't have to work tonight or tomorrow.

"You have to come. It's your birthday. You can't spend your twenty-first locked up in a room."

"Where's the party?"

Nathan's expression turns sly. "The KEN's."

"I'm in," I say quickly.

Nathan knew I wouldn't say no. The KENs are the most popular fraternity off-campus. They throw the best parties, and not everyone is invited. I always thought that if I pledged, they would be the right fit. With the number of classes I had, I didn't have the time to fit it in.

"Great! Maybe we can check out that strip club that just opened downtown afterward. You can have a lap dance. My treat." He tries to keep a semi-straight face.

They always tease me about my ability to chase women away, saying that a stripper is the closest I'll ever get to a real woman's touch.

"Yeah, that is not happening. Not tonight," I add, leaving my options open for later. I don't particularly like strip clubs, but I won't rule it out. "That's not really my idea of a good time. I think I do fine on my own. I have no problems getting the girl," I protest.

"I know. It's keeping the girl that's your problem." Garrett taunts as he walks up to us.

"And your problem is you have too many. We definitely don't envy you," I say to Garrett.

"Speak for yourself, man. What I wouldn't give…" Phil trails off as he approaches.

Nathan and I both shake our heads at the two of them. Like-minded and synchronized attitudes. They make the perfect roommates.

***

We arrive at the party fashionably late. The music is pumping, and the atmosphere is vibrant. There are a few people spread out around the place, some dancing in random spots. Voices float to my ears from every direction. I scope out the room full of people. It's the usual crowd that I've seen many times before. The KENs have endless snacks and drinks set up in the kitchen area. That's the focal point of the party for me tonight. I haven't gotten over my distaste for drinking but food…

"The ladies are definitely out tonight," Garrett declares beside me as he sizes up the probabilities.

The second he opens his mouth to speak, eyes began to turn in our direction. My friends marvel at the attention, unlike me.

"Hi, guys." Mandy saunters up to us, stopping directly in front of Garrett. She reaches up and throws one arm around his neck, then slowly drags her finger down to his chest. "Wanna dance?" She completely ignores the rest of us.

There are a few words I could use to describe Mandy, and subtle is not one of them. She's been after Garrett since we got here, and he strings her along like a sick puppy. I don't see how Garrett does it; all of the different girls coming and going. What's even worse is the girls knowing how he is and not caring.

"On that note, I will see you guys later," Garrett says to us. He lets her drag him away to who knows where for the rest of the night.

I excuse myself from Nathan and Phil not long after. I get something to eat and a virgin drink and find a spot outside to sit, away from the vultures. Normally when I come to these parties, I get involved. I dance and mingle. Tonight, I just want to listen to music for a little while and enjoy what's left of my birthday.

I find a comfy spot in one of the lawn chairs strewn about on the side of the house. There are a few passersby, but no one stops to bother me. I let my head fall back into a relaxed position when I'm done eating. I close my eyes and breathe in the pleasant night air. Over the music, I hear a distinct voice. It's alluring and one I've never heard before. There is something about it that makes my eyes pop open and search my surroundings.

I don't know why, but I stand when I locate the source of the voice. I can barely make out her outline from this distance in the dark. She's talking and laughing with another girl that I don't know. It looks like they are on their way out. *It would be a shame to wonder for the rest of my life about the one that got away*, I think to myself. It's my birthday. I figure why not do something spontaneous?

I take a couple of steps towards the two of them with one thing on my mind; finding out who the mystery girl is. I don't get far before a dark shadow crosses my path.

"What are you doing out here, man? The party's inside." Phil fights to get his words out.

I try to move around him to no avail. I look over his shoulder at the retreating figures. She's getting away, and Phil is about to make me lose my chance. I don't even know what she looks like. I'll have no way of finding her after this.

"Hey, where are you going? I just got here," he says, stepping in front of me again. He has obviously had a little bit too much to drink.

"I have to do…"

Phil grabs me in a headlock, cutting me off. I'm moments away from pummeling him. I manage to pry myself away and sidestep him, but it's too late. They're gone.

Chapter 24

Samantha

As soon as I got used to being at TVI, it was time for me to move on to Lakin. It was strange at first, getting used to a whole new set of faces and names.

My roommate, Emily, has been such a great help to me during my transition. She's teaching me the ropes and showing me where all of the hottest spots are. She took me to what she called an exclusive party last night. Her boyfriend, Calvin, is the Vice President of the fraternity. We didn't stay very long. It was basically a thirty-minute in and out, just enough to get my feet wet and introduce me to the hosts. Emily says that they are the most sought-after frat on campus. They know how to party, but they are also very active in the community. They are a very large organization and have a lot of influence outside of the university.

"Cool party last night, huh?" Emily comes in from her shower rustling her hair with the towel.

Emily is a morning person. I could set the alarm to her. We like most of the same things. She is more outspoken than I am, though. I normally sleep in an hour later on the weekends, but I'm up earlier than usual this morning.

"From what little I saw, yeah. Didn't you want to stay and be with Calvin?"

She waves my comment away. "I've gone to so many of those parties. They get old after a while."

"Aren't you worried about…" I pause unsure if I should be asking her this question. "About leaving Calvin alone with all of those girls?"

"Why would I be?" She chuckles softly. "Cal is a grown man. I trust him, and besides, he's just there because he has to be. He doesn't want to be there any more than I do. He's always said that the only reason he pledged is for the brotherhood and connections. He could care less about the girls and parties." She laughs again. "I often remind him that he met me at one of those parties. To which he says that was the day he stopped looking at all of the rest. My Cal is so sweet." She sighs and sits on the edge of her bed.

I'm still very leery of guys after what happened to me in high school. It's hard to trust anyone. I've only dated one guy since my split with Garrett. Harry was a normal guy, not too attractive that someone would want to steal him away. He said and did all of the right things. He opened doors and seemed genuinely interested in me. He was too perfect, and everything he did right, I couldn't help but wonder what his endgame was. I broke things off last year before he got too attached. I didn't feel right leading him on. I was leaving, and I knew there was no future for us. I admit that I didn't try to like him. I didn't want to like him. The only reason I agreed to date him in the first place is because of my Lacy. I told her I would try. I think Garrett ruined me. I'm broken. I don't know if I'll ever be able to feel again what I felt for Garrett.

"It's good that you have that with him," I tell Emily.

"Yeah, I got lucky, I guess." She shrugs her shoulder.

"What about you? Has anyone caught your eye since you've been here?"

"Ha," I respond in amusement. "I'm not looking for anyone. My experience with guys hasn't exactly been great."

"In what way?" she asks curiously.

"I'll just say that whoever manages to break down my wall will have to be a very special guy, like magician type special."

"There's nothing like getting your heart broken for the very first time." Emily gives me a sad but understanding look. "You can't dwell on that, Samantha. You need to get back out there, open up. I have been there and look at me. I found love again. You'll never know what's out there searching for you unless you are willing to accept it."

"You sound like my sister."

Emily perks up. "Your sister is a smart woman," she says matter-of-factly.

"Yeah." I smile with her and stand to go and take my shower.

***

TVI put in a good word for me at an affiliated restaurant here in Linkin. While I'm taking my business courses, I will also be training at Reynaldo's to be a Jr. Chef. They are one of the best southern cuisine restaurants in the city. For right now, I only work in the mornings to familiarize myself with prep work. Once I get the hang of things, they'll work me into the regular schedule.

Vivian, the head chef, is pretty cool. We clicked the first time that I met her. She's in her early fifties but doesn't look a day over thirty-five. Our first introduction was not a normal one. She took one look at me, and her first words were, *"You're gonna need a good hair net, honey."* Anyone else would have considered her rude for her improper greeting, not me. I remember holding back my chuckle because she could probably do without a hairnet but wore it so well. Her tiny half-inch curls were the first thing that I noticed about her. Her head is shaped perfectly, and her hair is styled in a way that I could never pull off.

"Alright, honey, I'll see you tomorrow," Vivian yells after me when it's time for me to leave.

"I'll be here bright and early," I respond before I walk out.

I told Emily I would pick her up after work. Calvin's car is in the shop, and he asked to borrow hers. Practice is on the playing field off-campus today, and he wasn't sure how long it would run since it's not the norm.

I pull up to the lot, find the closest park, and text Emily to let her know I'm here. I'm assuming practice hasn't begun yet. There's a group of guys gathered by the fence, bare-chested with shorts on. I spot Emily right away, talking to Calvin. She's the only girl around. She glances at her phone and looks around the parking lot. She points in my direction and whispers something in Calvin's ear that causes his lips to curl into a smile. He watches her as she walks away.

Emily climbs inside and huffs like she's just run a marathon. "Thank you for picking me up."

"It's no problem. I was out anyway."

I put the car in reverse, and as I'm backing out, I notice one of the guys throw the ball a little too hard in our direction. It lands a few feet away from the car. A dark-haired guy comes to scoop it up. He locks eyes with me, and his body goes still. The strangest feeling flows through me. He is a handsome specimen, and his eyes shimmer from a distance. I shake off the sudden spell.

"Who is that guy Emily… the one holding the ball?" I shift the car into drive and slowly press the gas. I don't know why, but I need my question answered.

"He's a looker, isn't he?"

I ignore her question. "Who is he?"

"His name is Bradley."

Bradley... His name reverberates inside my head. I struggle to look away from him, but I have no choice because I'm getting close to the exit. The air leaves my lungs when we break contact. I take a deep breath and refocus. I glance at Emily, who's watching me curiously.

"Do you want an introduction?" She asks.

"No," I say too quickly.

"Okay." I can still feel her eyes on me. "If you change your mind…"

"I won't." As much as I want to know more about him, I can't. It would be a mistake.

Chapter 25

Bradley

I tossed and turned last night, dreaming about the mysterious girl. Could that have been her with Calvin's girl? I couldn't see her face clearly or hear her voice, but the outline looked familiar. I need to find out for sure, or I'll go out of my mind. Every girl I've walked by since then, I wonder if she's the one. I won't know for sure unless I hear her voice again.

Calvin and I don't talk often, but he is the closest thing I have to a solution to my problem. I hope he doesn't think I'm crazy for what I'm about to do. I jog up to him after practice on Monday. I don't know what I'm going to say or how to present my predicament without being weird. I say the first thing that pops into my mind.

"Hey, Calvin wait up," I say as I approach him.

He stops walking and turns to greet me. "What's up?"

I stop next to him. *Good, he doesn't seem irritated or thrown off,* I think to myself. "I have a question to ask you. Who was that girl with Emily the other day?"

Calvin's lips curve into a smile. He crosses his arms over his chest. "What girl? You'll have to be more specific."

By the look on his face, I'm pretty sure he knows who I'm talking about and wants to give me a hard time about it. "The one that picked her up from practice on Saturday."

"Oh, that girl. Why do you want to know?"

"Just curious, I thought I had seen her somewhere before." It's not a total lie.

"She's Emily's roommate, Samantha."

"Did she transfer in from somewhere? I hadn't noticed her around campus until now."

"I think so. She's a junior. Emily has been showing her around. I just met her at the party the other night."

My interest is piqued when he mentions the party. My heartbeat picks up. I try to calm myself by thinking it could've been anyone. There is still a chance it may not be the right person.

"I could probably get Emily to introduce you if you want," Calvin speaks in a measured tone. "I'm headed over there later to drop something off. Why don't you tag along? Emily and I could set something up," he suggests.

I think about it for a moment. It's no different than what I was prepared to do at the party that night, right? "Don't you think that would be a little weird?"

"Not at all. I didn't snag Emily by not taking a chance. The worst thing that could happen is she says no, but at least then you'll know."

He's right. I've never shied away from anything but love. That's not what this is. I try to convince myself. *It's just a friendly meeting.* All I want to do is hear her voice.

Then maybe I can move on from this craze I'm going through. "Okay, set it up."

***

What have I gotten myself into? I just arrived at the frat house. I feel a little unease being here given the fact that Calvin and I don't really talk much. I appreciate him doing this for me, though. He's a standup guy. Calvin and Emily thought it would seem less suspicious if she came to him and brought her roommate along. I'll just happen to be here when they come.

I ring the doorbell, and Calvin answers and steps back for me to enter. "Come on in and make yourself at home. They should be here in a few minutes." He closes the door and ushers me to the sitting room where it's quiet. "You'll be more comfortable in here. The guys are in and out of the house all day. The front end of the house can get crowded and loud at times. Samantha thinks that Emily is only here to pick something up. We'll give you guys some privacy once they get here. So, make it count."

"Thanks, man. I appreciate this." I can't wrap my head around why he's doing this, but I thank him for it. I might not get the chance to meet her otherwise.

"Don't mention it. I'm always willing to help out those in need," he says with a grin.

I pick up the Car and Driver magazine from the table when I hear the doorbell sound. I need to do something with my hands and eyes. Calvin says something that I can't make out from here, and I hear laughter floating down the hallway.

"Do you mind if I speak with Cal for a few minutes?" I recognize Emily's voice right before they turn the corner.

"Sure, do what you need to do. I'll wait here."

It's the voice from the party. I would know it anywhere. It's really her. I look up slowly from the magazine that I'm pretending to read and lock eyes with her. For a moment, I think she recognizes me.

Emily clears her throat, and the girl looks away.

"We shouldn't be long," Calvin says to them. He nods his head in my direction. "This is my friend Bradley."

"I'm sure he wouldn't mind keeping you company until I'm through," Emily says to the girl. "Bradley, this is my roommate Samantha. You'll watch out for her, won't you? Keep the hounds away from her until I get back?"

I'm suddenly filled with confidence like I've never had before. "I'll be more than happy to."

She seems to flinch at my comment, but it doesn't deter me. I want to hear her voice again. I put the magazine down, stand, and walk over to her.

"Samantha, is it?" I ask her directly. I hold out my hand as a friendly gesture, and she stares at it. "It's okay, I don't bite," I say teasingly.

Her eyes snap up to mine. The way she squints at me is adorable. She finally takes my hand and shakes it firmly like this is a business dealing. I chuckle at her demeanor, which seems to irritate her more.

"Nice to meet you, Bradley." She says my name with mock interest.

"Okay… well, we will be back shortly. You kids have fun." Emily sings the last line as she pulls Calvin from the room.

"Can I have my hand back now?" I ask her after they've left.

She jerks her hand away and moves around me to sit on the couch opposite of where I was. Her posture is bone straight, and she watches me with frustration as I return to my seat. Her reaction fuels me to continue provoking her. The corner of my mouth lifts into what I hope is a cool smirk. I still don't get a reaction from her, other than her searing gaze. Her intensity matches my own, tit for tat.

"Are you from around here?" I ask her, kindly.

"No," she says curtly.

She's a beautiful girl. I was foolish enough to think that hearing her voice would be enough. I was wrong.

For the first time, since Val, I really want to know someone and not just anyone. I want to know Samantha. Not just her name and her interests; I want to know what makes her laugh and cry. I want to know her deepest secrets. I want to know what makes her tick and what turns her on, so that I can be the one to make it happen.

"May I ask where you're from?" She continues to stare at me. "The time may go by faster if we hold a conversation."

Her phone dings, and she lifts it to eye level to check it. Whatever she's looking at makes her giggle. Jealousy rocks through me. I want to be the one on the receiving end of that happiness. We sit in silence for a few minutes afterward.

She constantly raises her phone to look at it and continues to glance at the empty doorway. I assume she's checking the time. She probably thinks I'm rude for staring, but I can't seem to pull my eyes away.

After a while, she huffs out a breath and rolls her eyes, relenting to my question. "I'm from Hinton, Pennsylvania."

Relief flows through me at the sound of her vexed tone. I don't care that she sounds disinterested. Her attitude is actually doing weird things to me right now.

"Did you just move here? I've never seen you around before."

She readjusts herself in her seat. *She's loosening up*, I think to myself.

"Yes. I've only been here a few months." She glances at the doorway.

She looks as if she wants to bolt. I need to get her talking so I can hear more of her voice. "Do you like it here so far? Met any interesting people yet?"

That earns me a half-smile from her. "A few," she replies.

I wonder if I'm included in her list of interesting people. "Are you a first-year student?"

"I'm a special transfer."

I don't know what that means, but I'll go with it, as long as she's talking to me. "That sounds interesting. Maybe you could tell me all about it sometime."

"Knock, knock." Emily and Calvin enter the room with huge smiles on their faces.

I want to tell them to go away, that I'm not done yet. But then she will know that it was all a setup. Is it too soon to ask her out? I can't let this be the last time I hear her voice.

"Samantha, Cal and I were thinking..." Emily looks innocently at Samantha. "He and Bradley are about to go grab dinner. You and I haven't eaten yet. Maybe we can all go together?" She bats her puppy dog eyes at Samantha, pleading for her to say yes.

I want to shout yes for her. I don't know Calvin and Emily that well, but I love them for their effort.

"Please? It will be fun. It'll be a good chance for you to get to know someone other than me. Who better to start with than these two fine gentlemen?"

Samantha looks around the room at the three of us. Her gaze lingers on me for an instant longer than them. I can tell she doesn't like being put on the spot. For a moment, I think she's going to say no because of me.

"Okay. I'll go. I guess I can skip the noodles for one night." She turns her attention to Emily and gives her a genuine smile.

I remain calm on the outside. Inside, I'm an excited wreck that I get to spend more time in her presence. It's not a date, but before this night is over, I plan to ask her out, and hopefully, she will speak that three-letter word of acceptance.

Chapter 26

Samantha

It's been a long time since someone has infuriated me the way that Bradley does. Everything was fine until I got a glimpse of him and his chiseled abs. I didn't know he would be sitting in Calvin's house. I wasn't ready for the conversation that followed. I didn't have time to prepare for Bradley. He is so sexy, but he's not cocky, which makes it even worse. I'm feeling things that I don't want to feel. It's taking all of my willpower to sit across from him at this table and pretend that I don't feel the slightest tingle from his gaze… pretend that his voice is not as smooth as butter… pretend that the accidental brush from his hand earlier didn't cause the hairs on my arm to stand on end.

I don't even know this guy that won't take his eyes off of me. I do know that me plus him could lead to some very bad things. I can barely bring myself to look at him again. The barrier that I've built stands strong, but this guy… He has me wondering if I could get to know him without everything falling apart. What does he want with me? Wait, maybe I'm getting a little ahead of myself. We are just four people who happen to be hungry, eating dinner together.

Totally platonic and spur of the moment. *Why on earth did I agree to this?* I think to myself as I pick at my fries.

"You really love your ketchup."

I look up at Bradley when I hear his voice. "Hmm?"

"Ketchup… it must be a favorite. Should I be taking notes?"

Taking notes? For what? "No, my mind wandered off for a minute. I didn't realize that I was drowning the poor fry." I smile, and he chuckles at my comment.

Emily and Calvin left us sitting here to go pick out a song on the jukebox. Now they're swaying on the makeshift dance floor in the diner. My nerves are so screwed right now, that I can't even appreciate the sweetness of what they are doing.

"So, do you want to tell me all about that special transfer now?" Bradley asks.

Something in his voice makes me spill it. I give him a brief history lesson about my time at TVI and how I ended up here. He seems genuinely interested. His interest in me fuels me to want more information on him.

"Enough about me. Tell me something about you. How do you know Calvin?"

"I know Calvin from the football team."

"Oh? Do you play too?" I don't want him to think that I remember him from the other day. It might give the impression that I like him.

"Nah, the coach lets me practice with the team. I never joined. It's too big of a commitment."

So, he has commitment issues? I wonder to myself. It would be okay if he did. It's not like I'm looking for anything serious. Before I can fire off another question, he continues.

"I love the game, but it's not what I want to spend the rest of my life doing. My main focus is elsewhere." He smirks and looks me directly in my eyes. "I'm not afraid of commitment, not anymore. The boy that I was used to be afraid, but the man that I've become is far from it."

His comment traps me momentarily into thinking that it was meant for me. I clear my throat and shake the thought away. It wasn't directed at me. He's just stating a general fact. He just happens to be talking to me about it.

"If not football, then what is your main focus?" I ask him.

"I'm studying to be a mathematician."

"A mathematician? Really?" The tone of my question was all wrong. "I mean, that's great." I try to rephrase. I feel hot all over. Not only is he smoking hot, but he's also got the brains to match. He's not a true jock. This just keeps getting worse. My attraction to him is growing by the minute.

The vibration from his laughter reaches me from across the table. "I know… that's the reaction that I get from everyone when they find out what I want to do. I'm full of surprises." He leans up to whisper over the table. "FYI, I don't like them myself."

Note to self… he doesn't like surprises. Why would I even care?

He sits back. "In case you're ever thinking about throwing me a party or something." He answers my mental question. It's like he's reading my mind. That could be bad if he is.

"Why would I be thinking about throwing you a party?" I raise my brow in question. At the same time, I'm amused by his premonition.

"That's what people do when they're dating, right? They plan for birthdays and holidays. I figured I'd give you a head start on the small stuff. When you say yes, it's one less thing you'll have to worry about."

"When I say yes to what exactly?"

"To our second date."

"I wasn't aware that we had a first date."

He smirks like he knows a secret and leans closer to me. "Will you go out with me again?"

His question catches me off guard. I don't know what to say. If I say no, I feel like I would be letting Lacy down, but I know that saying yes would mean that I'm agreeing to try. I like him. There is something about him that won't let me speak the word no. I want to say yes, but would he be willing to take me as I am, with all of the broken pieces that can never be made whole again?

His eyes plead for my yes, and the flame inside of them won't let me say no. "Yes."

He sits back in his seat, satisfied. "Where should we go on our second date?"

"Second date?"

"Yes, you just agreed that this was our first."

"I did not."

I asked if you would go out with me *again*, and you said yes."

"You tricked me."

"No. I got you to admit what you already knew. I'm going to have fun getting to know you, Samantha." He begins to scribble something onto a napkin.

This guy... *I'm going to have fun getting to know you too, Bradley.*

He reaches over and places the folded napkin into my hand. It brings a smile to my face when I open it and read the note written down. *"Can I have your number, Samantha?"*

"You know, you could have just asked. I'm sitting right here."

"Yeah, I could have, but I wouldn't have gotten the same reaction."

I scribble my number down along with my added note, *'for emergencies only,'* and slide it back to him.

He reads it and looks up at me, one eye raised slightly higher than the other. A slow rumble comes from his chest. "I plan to have a lot of those."

Bradley pulls out his phone and saves my number inside and begins twiddling his thumbs across the screen. My phone dings. He watches me with expectant eyes. My skin heats at the message displayed. It's his number along with an invitation. *"Anytime, day or night."*

"Did anything interesting happen while we were gone?" Emily plops down in the booth next to me.

I feel like I've just stolen a piece of candy from the sacred dish, and it's time for me to confess. I open my mouth to reveal my secret, but the handsome hunk across from me beats me to it. I'm relieved when he opens his mouth to speak.

"Samantha just agreed to go out with me." Bradley grins from ear to ear.

"Smooth talker," Emily says to Bradley.

I blush from embarrassment. Bradley is a very smooth talker. My intent was not to like him. I had already made up my mind from the moment that I saw him. I would not give him the satisfaction that he so obviously wanted. I didn't care that his cheeks dimple when he smiles. All of that was thrown out the window the second he opened his mouth to speak. It didn't matter to him that I was trying to ignore him. He could care less that I had a plastered scowl. He didn't give up, and I finally gave in. I only hope that my giving into him doesn't come at a vast cost.

Chapter 27

Bradley

Why would anyone want to be a teacher? I wonder as the noise seems to follow me to my seat. I have a deep respect for people like Mrs. Matson, my public speaking teacher. She stands patiently by the blackboard with her fingers joined below her waist. Is her smile real, or is it something she feels like we need to see every day?

I take my normal seat near the back of the class and sit quietly until everyone else files in. Garrett sits to my left sandwiched between two girls. I shake my head in disbelief. They both lean towards him, whispering in his ear. Why would any girl want someone who obviously doesn't care at all what they think?

"Settle down class." Mrs. Matson claps her hands loudly twice. The sound echoes through the room.

A man walks in wearing a black suit and tie and goes to stand in the left corner of the room next to Mrs. Matson's desk. He has a small mustache and a three-inch beard. He looks to be about five feet seven inches. He has the same painted on smile as Mrs. Matson. Once everyone is seated, Mrs. Matson continues to speak.

"I have a treat for you this Friday. Today we have a surprise guest speaker. This is Mr. Adam Labenne from The Linkin Engineering Group."

This piques my interest. This is the company that I would like to work for when I'm done here. I've heard that it's very hard to land a job there. They only hire the best of the best. This could be my opportunity to gather as much information as I can and possibly gain a valuable contact.

"I'm going to step aside and let him have the floor now. Please give him your undivided attention class." Mrs. Matson motions for Mr. Labenne to take over. "Mr. Labenne, they're all yours."

I pull out a notebook and pen to take as many notes as I can. Most of the students seem uninterested. Some slouch down in their chairs. The quiet huffs can be heard over the silence. Only a few of us are excited about this lecture. That doesn't deter Mr. Labenne from his mission.

"Good morning, young adults. As Mrs. Matson stated, my name is Adam Labenne. I am the spokesperson for The Linkin Engineering Group. Before we get started, how many of you here are interested in a career in the engineering field?"

I raise my hand, along with five other students.

Mr. Labenne nods. "Great, I will be sticking around after school for anyone wanting more information and guidance."

He begins his lecture, and the ink spills onto my paper as he speaks. Getting this job would be a dream come true.

I meet with Mr. Labenne after school, where he goes more into depth about the field. By the end of the meeting,

I am confident that I will have no problems getting hired. He gives me his card and asks me to send over a transcript. After reviewing my record, he may even write me a recommendation letter.

***

My day keeps getting better and better. I send a text to Samantha, letting her know that I'm outside her dorm. I'm taking her to see '*Safe Haven.*' We talked briefly last night. She said she loves that movie and always wanted to see it on the big screen. I called around and found a place that displays old movies by request on a first-come, first-serve basis.

I stand outside the car and wait for her to come out. She seems surprised when she exits the building, and I open the car door for her.

"Hello, Samantha."

"Hello, Bradley." Her lips form a smile.

She settles into the car easily. I suspect that something is on her mind. Her hands grip the seat as I drive away. Her face becomes stoic. The last thing that I want is for her to feel uncomfortable around me.

It's been a few days since I've seen her. I keep glancing at her out of the corner of my eye. *What would her reaction be if I reach out for her hand?* She's quiet tonight; even more so than the last time we saw each other. I wonder what's going through that pretty little head of hers?

"Rough day?" I ask her, needing to hear her voice.

"No. I have a lot on my mind lately."

She looks at me and turns away. She doesn't explain any further. My guess is she's talking about me, or at least I hope so.

"Are you ready to tell me what the movie is about yet?" I had asked her over the phone last night, and she refused to tell me.

"That's not how this works."

"How does it work then?"

Her laugh is playful and infectious. "You sit down, watch the movie, ooh-and-aah, and be surprised by what comes next, just like everyone else."

"Don't you think that's a little unfair. You've already seen it."

"Yeah, and if I tell you about it, there is a good chance that you may not want to. Do you want to risk ruining our date?"

No, I don't, I think to myself. Nothing could ruin this date. I already know what the movie is about. I've caught glimpses of it while my sister was watching. It's cute watching Samantha try to explain, and now I know for sure that she's into this date. Otherwise, she would just tell me what the movie is about. That's what I would like to think. She could be using me just for that purpose. My plan is that by the end of tonight, she will want to see me over and over again.

We pull up to a gray stucco building with burgundy trimming. The sign out front says, Watcher's Theatre. I put the car in park and turn to face her.

"Okay, I give in. There is no way this is ending. One thing you'll learn about me, Samantha…" I lean closer to her.

She clears her throat, and her eyes widen with anticipation. "What's that?"

"I don't start something unless I'm positive that I can follow through."

My eyes hold hers for a few seconds, and she looks away. Her breathing is labored.

"We should go inside," she says in a whisper. Her gaze roams over the building when we exit the car. "Where did you find this place?" she asks as we approach the entrance.

"I asked around. I don't mind a little research, as long as it leads me to what I want." I shrug my shoulders. "It was time well spent," I say in the dark.

It's not a huge building, but it serves its purpose. It's unlike any other theatre I've seen before. It has six viewing rooms. Each room seats about fifty people. There is room for a small party in the back. The only thing that's the same is the large screen. The attendee informed us that they often rent the rooms out for celebrations and small private gatherings. It's a big hit with the younger crowds. I think it's a sweet deal. You pay for the room, pick the movie you want to watch, and they do the rest. We buy a tub of popcorn with extra butter, some chocolate covered almonds, and two drinks before we go inside.

Samantha and I have this room to ourselves for the next two hours. I hope it doesn't make her uncomfortable. I wave my free arm around the room. “It’s all ours,” I say with dramatic flair.

“It’s just the two of us… in here, alone?” she asks hesitantly.

“Yeah. If it makes you feel any better, I can sit on one side, and you can sit on the other.” I stare her down, praying that she doesn’t like that idea. “I’m a gentleman Sam,” I say, trying out a much shorter version of her name. Her face turns a cool shade of red at the sound of it. “I won’t do anything that you don’t want me to do. I promise.”

“No. We’re on a date. People on dates usually sit side by side at movies.” She looks around the room and points to a spot in the back of the theatre. “Up there. We’ll have the best view if we sit in the center.”

That was my thought too. I’m glad our thoughts mirror each other. That’s my favorite spot, all the way in the back. It’s the perfect vantage point and the darkest area of the theatre. I can see who’s coming in and going out. I imagine all of the mischiefs that can ensue under the protection of that darkness. I guess it’s a good spot for watching the movie too if that’s your main purpose.

“That was my thought exactly. Look at us, it’s only our second date, and we already think alike.”

She rolls her eyes and walks toward her desired area. Her laughter follows behind her. “You are too much.”

I follow behind her thinking. *You have no idea.* “So are you, Sam. So are you.”

I take the seat to her left. Sam offers me a true smile before her focus hones in on the movie. She watches the movie with great interest, and I watch her in the same way. It's not a bad movie, but I already know how their story ends. I would much rather give my attention to the beautiful young lady beside me.

There are many things about Sam that I don't know, like the way her mouth opens up for her small fingers to throw a popped kernel inside or the way her tongue snakes out to lick the butter from her lips. She takes small sips from her cup to wet her throat in between. I love her reserved giggles, like we're not the only two people here and her sentiment as she accepts the scene in front of her, all over again. Tiny tears drip from her eyes, and she wipes them away each time, not caring that I'm here sitting right next to her.

I take a chance and position my arm around her shoulders. She doesn't flinch away from me. Instead, she lays her head on my shoulder and nestles into my side. I don't know where this angel came from, but I'm not letting her go. I close my eyes momentarily and breathe in the sweet scent of her shampoo. Something inside of me screams, '*My Sam!*' She doesn't know what she has just done. With this one simple action, she nips at the most intimate part of me. She is arousing organs inside of me that lay dormant for years.

It's unlike me to shy away from anything. I will face this head-on without fail because I know deep down that she's my one. For the first time in my life, there is a small inkling of fear in the back of my mind. I've never been afraid like this before but Sam…

She makes me feel.

She makes me want.

She makes me believe.

I place a private kiss on the top of her head, so only I know it's done. She surprises me by taking my free hand in hers. I didn't know until this moment what would make my mom smile so brightly and put that sparkle in her eyes. Now I know… and I've only just gotten a sample.

Chapter 28

Samantha

I have never fallen so gracefully or been more comfortable with someone than I do with Bradley. This is a stark difference from the way things were with Garrett. Granted, I was a lot younger then and didn't know what the heck I was doing. The short amount of time that I spent with Harry doesn't compare either.

Holding Bradley's hand feels like the most normal thing in the world. I haven't felt this level of solace in a long time. I'm struck with disappointment when the movie ends, and I have to let go and remove myself from his embrace. He sat through the entire movie and never once protested. I knew he wasn't actually watching it. I could feel his eyes on me the entire time. Still, I appreciate this time with him.

We hold hands on the ride home. It's like we've done this all before. I can only imagine how flushed my cheeks are.

"So, did you like the movie?" I ask him slyly, knowing his attention was elsewhere.

The corners of his mouth arch up slightly. "I did, actually."

"Really? What was your favorite part?"

He's quiet for a few seconds, making me think that I've caught him in a lie.

"I enjoyed the whole movie, but what interests me the most is the talks she had with the dead wife. Now that, I did not expect. Things like that don't actually happen, do they? It's kind of creepy but cool."

Okay, now I'm totally confused. Maybe he was watching the movie. Could I have felt a vibe that wasn't there? I stare at the side of his face until a slow chuckle emerges from him.

"What? Are you surprised?"

"It's not that. I just thought… Never mind. I'm glad you enjoyed it." I smile at him and discreetly pull my hand away.

I don't know why hearing him tell me about the movie disappoints me. It shouldn't matter that I wasn't the center of his attention. That's not why we were there. But it does. A big part of me wants to walk away from Bradley and never see him again. I would probably be wise to listen to it, but I can't seem to shut out the smaller part that hides just behind the wall. The part that screams quietly within me... enable me to break free, let me feel, allow him to ruin me if that's what it takes to be with him. It's a low murmur that I fear will grow louder with every second that I spend with Bradley.

We pull up outside my dorm, and I say a quick goodbye and get out when he parks, leaving no room for more words. My body careens around into a firm set of arms before I can reach the front door. I'm unable to move my arms to object. Our eyes lock, and before I can utter a word, his lips connect with mine. My eyes close at the smoothness of his lips. I open up to let him explore my mouth. I relax in his arms and return the kiss.

All too quickly, Bradley pulls back and places his forehead on mine. His eyes are closed when I look up. I can't find the words to describe what just happened, and neither can he.

His eyes find mine again. His hands brush down my arms to linger in my hands for a moment. "Goodnight, Sam."

I watch him walk back to his car, too stunned to move or even speak. It's obvious that he's not leaving until I go inside. So, I turn and walk the other way. *I guess some things are better left unsaid.*

***

Emily is lying across her bed on her stomach with the phone pressed to her ear when I get in. I'm relieved that she's preoccupied. I wave, grab a pair of pajamas and take off to the shower. Thankfully, no one else had the same idea as me tonight. I set the water to lukewarm and step under the small shower head, grateful for the privacy. I savor the feel of the water cascading over my skin. My mind begins to wander to places it shouldn't go; into dangerous territory that could lead to my destruction, but the thought of it feels so good. I end my shower early, deciding that it wasn't the best idea after kissing Bradley.

Emily is leaning her back against her headboard when I get back to the room. I pull back my covers and get into bed, mimicking her position. I can see the curiosity written all over her face, but she doesn't know how to ask me.

Emily and I are friends, but we've only known each other for a few months. Topics like this still feel a little weird. It would be nice to have someone to tell my girlie secrets, though. We are tied to this rooming situation for the rest of the year, possibly more. She would be the obvious choice. She's nice enough, and she doesn't seem to mind telling me about her and Calvin. I guess it wouldn't hurt to spill my guts and get her opinion on things.

"Okay, what do you want to know," I ask her with a smile.

Her face lights, and she sits up straighter on her bed. "How did it go… with Bradley?"

"It went great. He took me to this diverse theatre. I didn't even know places like that existed."

"What movie did you see?"

"Safe Haven."

"Oh, I love that movie. Maybe next time we can double date."

My body shivers at the thought of the next time. I'm not even sure he wants to see me again. "Maybe," I say, unsure.

"That doesn't sound like a very good, maybe." She looks at me, confused. "I thought you said it went great."

"It did. He didn't mention another date, though. Perhaps he doesn't think it went as well as I thought."

She waves my comment away. "That doesn't mean anything. Guys are so strange in that way. You have to practically pry the information out of them most of the time."

I think about my time spent with Bradley. He has no problem offering up information. He willfully gives it away. Tonight, after we kissed, was different. His lips were sealed. Why do guys make everything so complicated? I can't blame him alone. It's my own fault for allowing him to suck me into this in the first place.

"I don't know, Emily. Bradley is a pretty straightforward guy. It's one of the reasons I agreed to go out with him." I don't mention the many other reasons that would most definitely make me seem completely shallow and easy.

I'm jostled by the unexpected ping of my phone. My privacy screen shows one message from Bradley. I open it up to read the contents, and a part of me quivers at his words.

Bradley: I thought about making an emergency call, but I think this is better for both of us. You've put a spell on me, Sam. I feel something tonight that I have never felt before. I hope you feel it too so that we can explore it together. If you don't, we should probably walk away now. The memory of our kiss is still fresh in my mind. I can't taste the sweetness of your lips again until you are ready for me, Sam, because once I do, there is no turning back.

Oh My God, what is he trying to do to me? I think to myself. I can't even bring myself to smile at his sentiment.

This is more than just a 'will you go out with me again' text. Bradley's message is very clear. He wants me... *all of me,* not just the physical. He wants me, mind, body, and soul. But how do I know that he's not wanting someone else the same way? There is no way to tell unless I get to know him, and that means I risk losing the shelter that I've so carefully built.

The one thing I'm sure of is the feeling that I now know we both felt... still feel. I'm inclined to explore this feeling with Bradley. I just don't know if I'm ready to accept the consequences.

I finally remove my eyes from the small screen to look at Emily. She's watching me with interest. Her eyes warrant an explanation.

"Bradley," I say to her. It's all I can manage. I have no idea what I'm going to do. I know what my impulse is telling me. My chest is tight from the push of my heart, trying to break free. I can't let it, not yet.

"What did he say?"

What's the best way to sum this up without going into detail? I want to burst into tears and, at the same time, laugh at my warring emotions. "He wants me to be with him."

Emily gushes with excitement. "Aww... And you were worried. I told you. He just needed to get his thoughts together."

I stare at Emily, wondering how she could be so happy at a time like this. Does the look on my face not say *crisis*?

She settles down and takes a good look at me. "What's the problem, Samantha? You don't look happy. I thought you wanted to be with him? Am I missing something here?"

I do want to be with him. That's the problem. I want to be happy about this, but not knowing the outcome is holding me back. "I wish there was a way to be sure."

"About what."

"The way things will turn out."

"I wish I had all of the answers too, but that's impossible. All you can do is figure out what it is you want and go for it. Nothing is always rainbows and roses."

"And what if going for it leads to me being hurt?"

She shrugs her shoulders. "You learn from the hurt, you grow, and move on. Hang on to the happiness that you felt and know that it's possible to feel that again. And who knows… the next time could be so much better."

"Thanks, Emily."

"Anytime," she says with a wink.

We turn out the lights and lay down. I release a long breath as exhaustion takes over me. I decide that I like talking to Emily about this stuff. She makes a lot of sense and reminds me so much of Lacy. I think I'm going to give Bradley a shot at breaking my heart… free.

Chapter 29

Bradley

Samantha: I feel it too. I want to try with you, Bradley, I really do.

I keep glancing at Sam's response to me from the other night. Something about her words leads me to believe that she's unsure. I can sense a 'but' somewhere that I dare not to question, out of fear that she will walk away.

We've both been busy this week with school and work. I haven't spoken to her since that night. She has agreed, via text, to go to the diner with me again tonight.

Garrett and Phil are crowded into my and Nate's room. The three of them are playing video games. Phil and Nate are on the controllers now. Apparently, it's the one thing that Garrett is not good at. He got kicked out before he barely got started.

Garrett leans toward me in an attempt to get a glimpse of my phone. "What are you looking at, man? You've been looking at that thing all morning. It must be important."

I lean away from him. "It is important," I say without explanation. "Nothing that would interest you."

Garrett studies me for a moment. "Oh, I see. It must be a female." His mouth forms a knowing smile.

My brows lift in question. "You're not interested in the ladies?" I ask, taking a jab at his ego.

He lets out a laugh. "Quite the contrary, my friend. I love the ladies, everything about them, from their heads down to their toes. Though not all toes are edible." He frowns slightly, which makes me laugh.

"What are you laughing at?" Nate twists his body in the same way as his character like it will make a difference.

"Garrett is telling me how good toes are. Have any of you tried them? I've never even considered it."

Nathan forcefully says, "Hell No!"

Phil, on the other hand, agrees with his roommate. "I have. The trick is to know how to tend to them just right. It makes the girls go wild. You shouldn't knock it until you try it. Trust me."

I would never trust Garrett nor Phil to teach me how to treat any girl. The way they behave is immoral, and I'm definitely not taking their opinion when it comes to my girl. Sam is too important to me.

"You're on your own with that one," Nate says.

Phil shakes his head from side to side.

"Moving on to more pressing matters," Garrett speaks over the rest of us. "There is a party tonight at the KENs. Anyone want to go?"

I smile to myself, thinking about the last party, where I discovered Sam. "You're on your own tonight. You'll have to find another chauffeur, or one of you will have to suck it up and take one for the team."

I haven't mentioned Sam to any of them before, not even Nate. He takes a quick glance at me before returning his attention to the game. "It's not like you to miss a KEN party."

His comment draws Garrett's attention. "Hot date?" he asks.

I smirk, knowing that there is at least one girl out there that he didn't get the chance to ruin. "Actually, I do. So, I'm sorry, but I'm sitting this one out."

Garrett smirks in that way that he does. "You're choosing a chick over us? I thought it was supposed to be brawn before beauty, or maybe it's bros before…"

"I don't agree with you there. None of that applies when it comes to this girl. She's different."

"So, what you're really saying is, you would rather hang out with her than wait around for us?" Phil asks in a teasing manner.

I shrug done with this topic. It's not going to matter what I say. They are intent on giving me a hard time about it.

***

Sam smiles as she approaches my car and climbs in. Gosh, it's good to see her again. I curse work and school for taking up so much of my time.

"Hi." Her eyes linger on my lips for a few seconds. She bites her bottom lip and looks up into my eyes.

My thoughts exactly, I think, as I remember how her lips felt against mine. “Hi. I hope you brought your appetite this time.”

“What do you mean, *this time*?” she asks, following a giggle.

“Well, the last time you had a vendetta against the fries if I remember correctly.”

She grins softly. “In my defense, the last time I was thrown into a situation that I wasn’t quite prepared for.”

“You feel different about tonight?”

“I do,” she says, looking me over cautiously. “I’ve been looking forward to this all day.”

“I think that’s my cue to get this started then.” My eyes purposely roam over the length of her curvy figure before I drive away.

“Do you mind if I put the window down? I love the smell of the night air.”

Something flashes in her eyes, and she quickly shakes it away. I want to ask what that thing is, but I can tell she doesn’t trust me completely yet. She wears her shield like a second skin. I couldn’t see it clearly at first, but the more I get to know her, the more lucid it becomes. I understand her need to be cautious. I’ve been where she is. I’ve been leery of letting anyone get close to me in my past. So, I get it. I have to get her to let me in and tell me what or who made her this way. I want to help her move past everything that’s ever hurt her. I plan to replace her bad memories with the good.

“Sure, go ahead.”

She sucks in a long breath as the wind blows across her face. It's hard to keep my eyes focused on the road. I envy the way her hair flutters around her neck, a few strands reaching down to tease the soft curve of her breast. She is a beautiful sight to see. If I wasn't driving and her wall didn't stand between us… I can only imagine the things we could do to pass the time.

She turns her head towards me. A slow smile creeps up, and I know that I've been caught, but I don't care. I want her to know that she is at the center of my thoughts. I want her to feel comfortable with me, enough that I become her second skin.

"See something you like?" she asks playfully, batting her lashes.

"Are you flirting with me, Sam? That's a dangerous game you're playing. I might get the wrong idea."

Her face becomes a shade darker. She leans closer to the window to let the air cool her flustered skin. She's silent for the rest of the drive. I hope that my comment didn't ruin the small progress I have already made.

We walk side by side up to the diner's door. I pull it open and motion for her to go ahead of me. "You can pick the spot."

She leads me to a table by the window, much smaller than the booth we were in the last time. We're sitting across from each other, but the size of the table makes this feel much more intimate. I already know what I want, so I don't bother looking at the menu. Sam picks hers up to browse through the options.

"Hi, I'm Betty, and I'll be your server tonight. What can I get you kids to eat?"

We both look up at the older woman, who I remember from the last time. Her pen taps gently against her notepad as she waits for our response. She kind of reminds me of my grandma with her color rinsed curly hair and untanned skin.

"Ladies first," I say to Sam.

"I'll have a quarter-pound cheeseburger with fries…" she pauses to glance at me. We share a knowing look and smile at the memory. "... And a small lemonade, please."

"And for you, young man?" Betty looks at me, expectantly.

"I'll take the half-pound bacon burger with extra bacon and cheese fries."

"Anything to drink with that?"

"Bottled water, please."

"Will that be all?" Betty asks.

"We may want dessert later." I glance over at Sam. "Can we have some extra ketchup? My girl here is a big fan."

Sam bursts into laughter at our private joke. I knew that would get a reaction out of her. This is the first time I've heard her laugh that way since that first night at the party.

"Kids." Betty shakes her head and mumbles something incoherent as she walks away.

Sam quiets down and clasps her hands together on top of the table. She gives me a hesitant look, and that unknown entity flashes in her eyes again.

"Did I miss something, Bradley?"

I'm confused by her question. "What do you mean?"

"Your girl?" she inquires.

I lean forward and pull her hands apart. I hold them within my own. Her warmth slinks into my hands, filling the chilled crevices of my skin. I look deeply into her eyes in search of understanding and acceptance. "I thought I was clear about what I wanted the other night."

She continues to stare at me without uttering a word. Her fingers twitch under my hold.

"Let me spell it out for you, Sam. This thing between us, whatever it is, is not a game to me. It is not my intention to use you and throw you away. My ultimate goal is to know all of you better than you know yourself. I want to get under your skin and live there with you, Sam. So, to answer your question… Yes, you are my girl, unless you think otherwise."

A long silence stretches between us. She doesn't say the words, but her eyes speak to me without her permission. They paint a jagged picture of compliance and apprehension, all wrapped up in a loosely cemented frame.

"Okay, kids. We have one quarter with fries, extra ketchup, and one half-pound with extra bacon and cheese fries. One lemonade and one bottled water." Betty's seasoned voice breaks through the silence. "Let me know if you kids need anything else."

Sam pops a fry into her mouth when Betty walks away. She still hasn't said anything. I take that as a sign that she's not ready yet and needs more time to think. We eat our food in silence between the stolen glances and tension.

"Talk to me, Sam," I say when we are done eating. "Tell me something about you that I don't know. What's your favorite color and favorite food? What do you like to do for fun? How many…"

"Hold on there ranger." She grins around her words. "One question at a time. What do you want to know first?"

"I'll take whatever you want to offer me."

"Yellow is my favorite color."

I would never have guessed that. I haven't seen her wear anything yellow since we met. I was leaning more towards green. "Why yellow?"

"It reminds me of the sun. It's bright and powerful. It attracts attention and, at the same time, commands you to look away. Can you imagine having the authority to make something gravitate towards you and pull away, all in the same span?"

"I can imagine." That color suits her very well. She has that power over me. Only I refuse to pull away. I've never put so much thought into a single color before. To hear her explain it to me, it makes perfect sense.

"I don't really have a favorite food. Though I do enjoy my fries and ketchup." She grins, and I laugh along with her.

I could listen to her talk forever.

"Let me see. Oh yeah, fun… I haven't had fun in a long time. Not counting my time with you, of course. I don't really get out much."

"Why is that?"

"I've been concentrating all of my time on school and work, and besides that, I don't know many people here."

"So, there is nothing that you like to do? Not even when you were in high school?"

Sam turns her head to peer outside. Her face looks pained. I hate seeing that look on her face.

"High school was…" her smile contradicts the sadness in her eyes when they meet mine. "I learned a lot in high school. I did a lot of things that I wish weren't tied to certain memories."

I've never had my heart broken, but I know the signs. Whoever this person was that hurt her, deserves to suffer. They need to feel the same hurt that they caused her.

I angle my head to match her gaze. "Someone hurt you."

Her mouth opens and shuts several times. She closes her eyes, inhales and exhales slowly. When she looks at me again, her eyes are still sad and soft, but I can see a hardness behind them, mixed with determination and distrust.

She nods her head, yes. "I was in a relationship with this guy in high school. I put all of my trust in him. What a huge mistake that was. He felt like I wasn't giving him enough of my time. So, he cheated on me and basically told me it was my fault."

She stops talking, and her eyes assess me as if she's waiting for me to react. I hold her stare, surprised that she's disclosed any of this to me at all.

"Look, the only reason I'm telling you this is because I want to get to know you, and I want you to know me. In order to do that, there can be no secrets. For you to know me, first you must understand me and why I am the way that I am. I don't want to be hurt like that again."

I watch her, wishing that we were close enough for me to pull her into me. I want to replace that look in her eyes with something greater than she could ever imagine.

"I know it won't mean much to you now, Sam, but I'm not that person. I would never disrespect you. Given enough time, you'll see that all I want is to make and keep you happy."

Now that she's opened up to me, I finally feel like we're moving forward. There's still a huge obstacle in my way, and I know she won't make it easy for me, but my life has not always been easy. Sam is the most significant challenge I've ever faced. It's my purpose to convince her that we are worth trying for.

Chapter 30

Samantha

People always tell you how easy it is to fall in love, but no one ever tells you how hard it is to resist. Everyone can't be searching for love. There has to be someone like me, someone who has been hurt before and can tell me how they did it. How do you resist the fall when you feel the other half of your heart is right in front of you?

Brad came out of nowhere, and he's slowly nipping at my wall. With every day that passes, there's a new crack, another point of entry that requires a patch. He's wearing me down, and I'm running out of excuses.

In the past month, between all of the hand holding and touching, I've started to feel things. I knew I could deal with the physical before all of this started, but the emotional connection that's ever-present, I wasn't prepared for. It's unlike any feeling that I've ever felt, and it frightens me.

Brad frightens me.

He frightens me to the point where I need a break. It's not because he's a bad guy. It's because he's too good at everything. Bradley is my yellow. I've tried not to get too close and have failed miserably. I need time to think. I want to talk to someone that's totally removed from our relationship. I have to pull myself away from the rough hands that slink their way around my belly so that I can see clearly.

"How's that, Sam? Is that convincing enough?" Brad's mouth is inches away from my ear. His torso is flush against my back, and I'm melting from the inside out.

"This isn't the time or the place to prove me wrong, Brad." It was foolish of me to challenge him, knowing that he would wait until we were in a public place to accept. He's told me several times, *"I don't care who knows you're my girl. Let them watch."* I thought it was just a figure of speech until now.

He asked me to go to the amusement park and suggested that we get on the biggest roller coaster there. I told him that he'd have to convince me. Now we're standing in a crowd of people, next to 'The Terror,' and his method of persuasion is so hard to resist. How do I say no to this? I'm beginning to wonder if anyone has ever said no to Brad.

"It's the perfect time," he says while teasing my ear with the tip of his nose.

I feel like all eyes are sharing this intimate moment with us. "Okay, you've coerced me into it. You don't play fair."

Brad chuckles and steps back, breaking our contact. "I never promised you I would."

I look over my shoulder at him in mock disbelief. "But you did promise to protect me from dangerous things. I think this qualifies as a dangerous thing."

"And I will protect you while we're on it. I promise that if something happens to you, it happens to me first."

"That's not too reassuring."

"Trust me. It will be fun." He takes my hand again and leads me on.

Something happens to me when Brad wraps me in his arms. I forget every ounce of fear that I felt before getting onto this ride. I feel safe sitting next to him, even as I scream at the top of my lungs on the way down.

Brad smooths down the wild strands of my hair and smirks at me when we get off. He did what he said he would do. I'm safe. As much as I don't want to admit it, the ride was fun.

"That wasn't so bad, was it?"

I can't think straight when he's touching me. I'd agree to anything as long as his hands are on me. "I guess not."

Brad's eyes turn serious. "I'm going to kiss you now," he warns me.

Even with his warning, I don't see it coming. His lips come down on mine and submerge me like we are the only two people here. I should be embarrassed or maybe a little mad, but I can't be upset with him for being true to his word.

"I don't care who knows you're my girl. Let them watch."

***

'Screwed' only begins to describe my position. All it takes is a couple of hours for me to miss him. The book that I listened to on the way to my dad's house was only a distraction. As soon as it's taken away, the feeling starts to creep in. I try to push it aside, but that doesn't help, and soon realization starts to set in. I'm the one thing that I didn't want to be, and there's not much of a wall to hold on to.

The familiar smell of home hits me the moment I open the door. "Dad!" I call through the house, not wanting to alarm him.

Lacy rounds the corner, stopping me in my tracks. Dad knew I was coming, but I wasn't expecting Lacy to be here. I'm surprised and happy to see her.

"Hi, Grace!" She gives me the biggest hug and steps back to look at me. Her eyes squinch, making me feel guilty for keeping a secret. I know she senses something is off. I could never keep anything from her. She's always been able to tell with me.

"Hey! What are you doing here?"

"Dad told me you were coming. You know dad. He got all excited and had to tell me. There is no surprise visit unless you keep it from dad too." She pulls me into the living room and down to the couch. "How long are you here?"

"Just through the weekend." Classes aren't scheduled until Tuesday, but after this long drive, I'll need Monday to rest up. "Where's dad?"

"He had to run an errand. He should be back soon." She grabs hold of my hand. "I want to know everything. How is school?"

"School is good. I've managed to hold on to my perfect GPA and have a little bit of fun. Emily, my roommate, has familiarized me with the place. She gives really good advice too. She kind of reminds me of you."

"Really? I'm glad you found someone to stand in for me since I can't be there."

"She can never take your place, though. You give the best advice." I don't know how to spring my news on her.

She smiles knowingly. "You can tell me about him, you know."

How does she always know? I think to myself. "I… I'm sorry, Lacy. I wanted to tell you when I first met him, but something inside of me kept thinking what's the point. It won't last anyway."

"How did you meet?"

I grin inwardly, wondering what Lacy will think of my answer. "We met at a frat house."

Her brows shoot up, and for a second, I think she's going to judge me. "A frat house? How did that happen?"

"My roommate, of course. She's in a relationship with one of the guys and thought it would be a good idea to introduce me to the group. They are very influential."

"So, this guy… what's his name? What is he like?"

"His name is Bradley. He's smart and kind and funny..." Describing Brad warms me inside. He's a part of me now, and his essence follows me everywhere. How did I get here?

Lacy watches me closely like she always does. She dissects every word and body movement until she finds what she's looking for. "You're in love with him." She states a matter of fact.

"I'm scared, Lacy. I didn't mean for this to happen. It's the last thing I wanted but Brad..., there is something about him that makes me forget everything. I can't think straight around him. I've loved before, but not like this. Brad is different. He's all-consuming. I tried my best to keep him at a distance, and he was determined that I wouldn't."

"Oh, Grace," she says with eyes full of understanding. "It's okay to be a little afraid. I've been married for a few years now, and I get scared sometimes too. Love is a fickle thing. There's no way of knowing what comes next. But you know what? That's the beauty of it. Focus on the way he makes you feel in the present. Try not to think so much about what may be. He sounds like a nice, respectable guy."

"He's perfect, Lacy. That's what scares me the most. I can't find a single flaw. Something has to be wrong, right?"

"Don't overthink it. His flaws will surface soon enough." She chuckles. "I can see behind all of your doubt that he makes you happy. You're practically glowing. Concentrate on that."

Lacy is one of the few that I trust most in this world. If she says everything will be okay, I have to believe it. She would never steer me wrong. I'm glad she was here when I arrived. I feel better after our talk.

"Thanks, Lacy."

"Anytime sis. I'm glad you took my advice. It's good to see you happy again. You'll have to bring Brad for a visit one day; sooner rather than later."

"I'll think about it."

She pulls me in for a hug. I don't know if Brad and I are at the 'meet the family' stage yet. Neither of us has uttered the L word to the other. Does he even love me, or is he still figuring it out?

Chapter 31

Bradley

I'm sure I'll be staying in Linkin after I graduate, but I still want to explore my other options. I invited Sam along for the weekend. She accepted, but I can tell she's nervous about it. We'll be completely alone for the first time since we started dating. I admit I'm a little anxious myself. It's been over three months since I met her, and I can't wait to finally have her to myself. Tonight, I want to get to know every single part of her; if she'll let me.

She's been acting strange since her visit home last week. She barely said anything during the one-hour drive here. I asked her about it, but she brushed it off, saying, *'I'm fine.'* I know she's not fine. Something is bothering her. Hopefully, this weekend she can relax enough to tell me what it is. I'll get it out of her one way or the other.

"Hi, how are you today?" Todd, the young man behind the check-in desk, greets us cheerfully when we step in front of him.

"Fine, and you?" I say in return. Sam smiles but doesn't speak.

"Are you checking in to the resort this evening?"

"Yes. Reservation for Bradley Pierce, party of two."

"Okay. Give me a moment to look you up."

I glance at Sam while he's clicking away on his keyboard. Her gaze is focused on the wall in front of us.

"Here you are. I just need the credit card you made the reservation with and your ID for security purposes."

I hand over my card and driver's license. He verifies the information and gives them back to me with two key cards to our room.

"Do you need any help with your bags?"

"No. I think we can manage," I say.

"Well, if you need anything else, you can reach the front desk by dialing zero from your room. Enjoy your stay Mr. & Mrs. Pierce."

Sam's eyes widen at Todd's comment. It's the first real reaction I've seen from her since we began this trip. I'm not phased at all. I like the sound of that. I look forward to the day when I can proudly call her my wife. It's hard to know if she feels the same, though. I wonder if her shocked expression was a good or bad thing. Either way, I don't correct him.

"Thank you. I'm sure we will." *I'm going to make sure of it.* I grab Sam's hand and lead her to the elevators.

The condo is beautifully decorated. The warm hues of blue, tan, and grey provide a homey feel. There's a small living room, a full kitchen and one bedroom with a full bath. I doubt if we'll get much use out of the kitchen. *Unless Sam decides she wants to play.*

"What's so funny?" she asks.

I hadn't noticed her watching me until she said something from across the room. "I could tell you, but you may not approve." I wiggle my brows at her playfully.

"Who knows…?" she shrugs. "My approval rate, when it comes to you, is getting higher by the day."

That's the Sam that I know; hopeful, flirtatious, sexy and modest. My Sam… she doesn't even have to try. She turns and bends over to get something out of her bag. My head tilts on instinct to look at her curves. I hope she doesn't make me sleep on the sofa tonight.

"I can feel you watching me, Brad." Her voice sings across the room. She chuckles under her breath.

Her teasing only encourages me further. I've learned that the only way to get through to Sam, is to go straight up; no curves, no turns… no chaser.

"I must be doing something right then," I say as I creep up behind her. I lay my palms flat against the contours of her hips. She jumps to attention and nearly tips over before I catch her and swing her to face me.

"Brad!" She whisper-shouts my name with bated breath.

I pull her closer to me and trap her in my arms. "Yes, Sam?"

Her eyes, full of want, hold mine. "I'm going to kiss you now." She says the words I've said to her countless times before, and I have no objections.

Our lips meet slowly, and I let her take the lead. Her tongue slips through the thin slit between my lips, requesting entry. This is the first time that she has taken the reigns. It's a turning point for us. I know that she's finally accepting this thing between us. I can feel it in her movement, the urgency of her kiss, and the way her hands tangle in my hair. I've felt it coming for a long time, and now I can finally admit it. I'm in love with Samantha Young, and I know she loves me too. Her actions say so much more than her words ever could.

We pull apart slowly. Her eyes are soft and pleading for me to see the truth within her. A single tear slips down her cheek, and I wipe it away with my thumb. It's the first time that I've ever seen her vulnerable. My heart swells with pride. I shouldn't feel pleasure in what she probably sees as a failure, but I do. Not because it feels good to see her cry; I would never want that. I'm happy because, with that single tear, I know that I've finally torn down her wall.

I look deep into her eyes and say the words that I know to be true. "I'm in love with you, Sam."

Her forehead falls to my chest. Her tremors vibrate through me. I never meant to make her cry. I scoop her up into my arms, carry her over to the bed and lay her down gently. I climb in behind her and wrap my arms around her. We stay like this for a while before her subtle movements begin to slow, and her body stills. I breathe in the perfume of her hair and snuggle in closer, being careful not to wake her.

We're both tired from the drive, and I've just tossed a loaded thought into her head. It's no wonder she crashed. I don't have my visit until tomorrow. So, I'm all hers for the rest of the night.

I take an hour nap and wake before she does. It's strange waking up next to her. She's still sound asleep. Her breathing is even, and she doesn't move when I get up. I kiss her temple and smile down at her. Neither of us has eaten since this morning. There's nothing here to cook and I would rather us stay in tonight. I have an idea that could lighten both of our moods.

I order room service and ask that it be delivered in about thirty minutes; just enough time for me to enjoy a shower and release my rising tension.

After my shower, I wrap a towel around my waist until I can get the clothes from my bag. I halt at the bathroom door but only for a few seconds. The erection that I rubbed out during my shower creeps right back in, erasing what little progress I'd made.

Sam is sitting upright on the side of the bed. Her eyes roam the length of me and land on my lips. It's obvious that our minds are running at parallel speed. As much as I want to take her right now, I hold back. I refrain from sucking on her bottom lip that she's now biting and running my fingers over the curve of her breast. There's plenty of time for that after we eat.

"Hey, beautiful. Did you sleep well?" I ask her, breaking through the rigid silence.

"Best nap I've ever taken." Her eyes follow me as I sit down beside her. "How was your shower?"

"It could have been better if I had some company."

She wrings her hands together in her lap, causing a smirk to appear on my face. Her nervous energy skims my senses.

It's all because of me that she feels this way. She's not usually this way with me, but considering I'm sitting next to her practically naked, it's understandable. For now, at least. I don't want her to be nervous in the bedroom. I want to see her everyday confidence to thrive, regardless of the situation. That's one habit I look forward to breaking. *Later*, I think to myself. I can't bear to touch her right now, but oh how my hands long to do bad things.

With that thought, my head gravitates toward the sweet spot behind her ear without my permission. Before I can make contact, there's a knock on the door. We both startled at the interruption.

"Are you expecting someone?" She looks at me, expectantly.

"I ordered us room service. I hope that's okay."

I'm halfway to the door before I realize I don't have any clothes on and stop.

"Would you mind getting that while I throw on some pants?" I ask her.

"What's the matter? Afraid of a little ogling?" She wiggles her brows at me.

"Not at all. I'm doing us all a favor. Can you imagine the look on the attendant's face if my towel were to drop?"

Her eyes move to the slightly raised cloth around my waist. She licks her lips, and her skin flushes crimson before her gaze has a chance to return to my eyes. *In due time Sam. You won't have to wonder for long.* I clear my throat to get her attention.

"Sam?"

She takes the tip from my hand. "The door, right."

Her words are jumbled, and I love every minute of this. It's going to be fun getting to know the wilder side of Sam.

"Mrs. Pierce. Are you enjoying your vacation so far?" The man at the door greets Sam in the way that I like.

She doesn't skip a beat. "I am, thanks for asking."

Their voices trail off when I enter the bedroom. I quickly slip on some sweats so that I can get back to her. I want to see the look on her face when she opens up the top on the tray. I walk out just in time to see her hand over the tip before they exit. I walk up behind her in the center of the living room and wrap my arms around her. My lips finally make contact with her sweet spot. I nip at her earlobe. Air rushes from her lungs. I can feel her body relax against me.

"Sam, are you as hungry as I am?"

"Am I hungry?" She answers my question with her own.

"Yes, hungry," I say again.

"I'm starved." Her voice is barely audible.

"We should eat then." I step back and unwrap myself from her. She sucks in a deep breath at the loss of contact.

"Yeah, we probably should." Sam's gaze is full of fluster and disappointment when she turns to look at me.

The muscles in my chest flex involuntarily at the sight of her reddened skin. I should have put on a shirt and kept my distance. I shouldn't have touched her again until we were both ready. I've never wanted anyone as bad as I want her. I'm in love with the object of my affection.

Chapter 32

Samantha

I burst into laughter at the tray of fries and the huge bowl of ketchup next to it. I can't believe he did this. The workers probably think we're crazy. He ordered burgers and chicken tenders too, but still, it's funny.

"I thought you might enjoy this. It was meant to make you laugh. If you want something different to eat, I can reorder."

"Not a chance. You did good."

"Well, in that case, let's eat." He rubs his hands together swiftly.

Those hands... I think to myself. The same hands that were all over me, not even five minutes ago. The hands that I long to feel again.

We ditch the table and opt for the couch in the living room. The two-foot gap between us is not nearly enough to calm the energy flow. I wonder if it's just me or if he feels it too. I grab a fry, dip it in the ketchup, and pop it into my mouth to keep myself from saying anything that may incriminate me.

He watches me with interest. His stares don't make me bashful anymore. If anything, I crave them. I yearn for the slow burn that follows his eyes across my body.

"How is it?" he asks me.

"It's tasty… satisfying." I pop another fry into my mouth, realizing how my words could be misconstrued. On the inside, I scold myself for allowing the vixen in me to say exactly what's on her mind. I also blame the guy in front of me for blocking out my filter. I can't seem to turn it on around him.

"Is that so?" His lips quirk at the corner, making me squirm inside.

"Mmhm."

I pick up the burger and take a huge bite and another, and another, thinking that the more I have to chew, the less I'll have to say. Looking at Brad now, that was the wrong move. I can see the cloud in his eyes and sense his thoughts. He eats quickly, takes a drink, and sits back on the couch, throwing his arm around the back. He continues to watch me until I'm done eating.

"What do you want to do now, Sam? The night's yours."

I can think of a few things. That's what I want to say, but I refrain. I want to know where his mind is, where he thinks this relationship is going before I dive in too deep.

"Would you mind if we just talk?" I ask hesitantly.

"Not at all. What's on your mind?"

"Earlier, you told me you're in love with me."

He nods his head, approvingly, and smiles. "Yes, I am."

"I know what I expect that to mean, but what does that mean to you, Brad? How are you so certain?"

He cautiously moves closer to me, erasing one foot of space. "It's quite simple, actually. You are my yellow Sam. Before every lifelong decision that I make, I think of you. You're a part of me now. You make me feel something so real and terrifying, but I don't want to run away from it. I want to embrace it regardless of how much it may burn."

Your Yellow? "Why would you even want to continue, if there's any chance you might get hurt?"

He scoots even closer, erasing what protection lay between us. He takes my hand in his. "How can I not?" he asks. "I've spent years of my life being afraid to fall in love, all because I was too young to understand it. I'm not that kid anymore, Sam. I've learned a few things in my old age."

I can't stop the giggle that spills out of me. "You are not old."

"Maybe not, but I am wiser. I'd be a fool to let you slip through my fingers, and I would never forgive myself if I don't try."

I have spent years of my life loving, but I didn't truly know what it meant to fall until Brad happened.

"Brad?"

"Yes."

"I'm going to kiss you now."

I thought that's what I was going to do. Only this time, Brad takes the lead. He moves in slowly for a kiss, and when our lips touch, my heart flutters out of control. He pulls me onto his lap to straddle him. I've never been in this position before or in any position. I want him to have me in whatever way he deems fit. One more thing that frightens me, because I have no idea what I'm doing. If we continue like this, we're headed straight to that unfamiliar place.

I break away from him. "Brad," I say breathily. "I need to tell you something."

His firm hands hold my waist as his eyes meet mine. "Is everything okay?"

"It's fine, but…" My voice trails off as I think of a way to explain. Everything about Brad screams 'experienced.' How do I tell him that I'm not, and will he still want me when he finds out? "I've never been with anyone before." I move my gaze away from him, not wanting to see the disappointment in his eyes.

I close my eyes at the touch of his finger, guiding me back to him.

"Open your eyes, Sam."

I prepare myself for his refusal and open my eyes to look at him. I feel a slight twitch from him below me.

"That is the sexiest thing that I've ever heard."

The twitch comes again, and I think about moving away, but Brad's hold on me is steadfast.

"I want you, Sam, in every way, but I won't go through with this unless you're ready." The back of his hand smooths down my cheek. "Are you ready, Sam?"

"Yes."

He takes my yes and stands with me in tow. I clamp my legs around his waist as he walks us to the bedroom. He stops beside the bed to let me down and turn the covers back.

I've never experienced nervousness, excitement, and fright all at the same time before. He takes his time undressing me. "Lay down," he says in a soothing voice.

I ease onto the center of the bed, bracing myself up on my elbows to watch him undress. His eyes never leave mine. I see that he's more than ready for this as he rolls the protective shield onto his rigid length. I lay flat on my back when he climbs on top of me. His lips tease the sensitive spot behind my ear, causing me to shiver. He peppers my skin with sweet kisses down to my breast and sucks gently on the supple buds, paying special attention to each one. I moan quietly with every soft pinch from his lips.

"Brad… please."

"You like that," he says as a fact.

"Yes, more."

His tongue makes a trail down to my belly button and even further until he reaches unchartered territory.

He looks up at me with hungry eyes and words I never would have expected in this position, spill from his mouth. "I'm going to kiss you now."

I tangle my hands in his hair as he explores a part of me that's only ever been touched by me. His mouth makes a quiet, smacking sound. He licks his lips and makes a trail back up the center of my body. His eyes search mine asking for permission to continue, and I don't say a word. He takes my silence as consent and reaches down between us. I take a quick peek at him, wondering how something that big is going to fit inside of me.

I can't help myself. I want to know. "Will it fit?" The question slips out of my mouth, and I slap myself mentally.

Brad smirks slyly. "I'll take it slow. Just relax." He brushes my center with the tip of his shaft. "If I hurt you, call out my name."

He enters me slowly, and my body tenses in response. Somewhere between the third and fourth stroke, I began to relax, and the pain turns into pure pleasure. I've never felt anything like it before. I claw at the strained muscles in his back. I don't want him to stop. I want more.

"Brad." I cry out his name in a whispered breath, and his body goes still.

"Sam? Am I hurting you? Do you want me to stop?"

"No, please don't stop," I say, already missing him. I don't understand this feeling. How can I miss something that's still planted firmly inside of me? "Don't stop."

Brad continues his movement at my command until something inside of me convulses around him, begging him to join me, wanting him to experience the same bliss.

Afterward, we lay facing each other, both of us breathing heavily. His fingers brush the loose strands of my hair behind my ear. His eyes are so trusting and full of love. They show no signs of wanting to turn and walk away.

I reach up and place my palm on his cheek, wondering how I got here. I tried so hard to keep this from happening, and in the end, it didn't work.

"I'm in love with you, Bradley Pierce."

He pulls me closer to him and places a lingering kiss on my forehead. I close my eyes on contact and contemplate the expanse of my fall.

Three months…

That's how long it took me to fall in love with Brad.

I opened up.

I let him in.

I gave him an inch… And he took the extra mile.

He listens to me and laughs at my bad jokes. I'm drawn to him in ways I can't describe. My heart beats wildly at the thought of him. I can't stop the onset of butterflies and shivers whenever he is near me. I can now see a future where that space once lay empty.

Three hours…

The time between our arrival until now.

Within this span, Brad has crumbled what was left of my wall.

He invited me here with him. I knew deep down that I wouldn't be able to resist him. I knew that he would break me. Yet, I came anyway. He challenges me at every turn, and his teasing is driving me insane. As if that wasn't enough, he answered a question that's been at the forefront of my mind. He's in love with me. That's the thing that finally caused my shelter to topple over.

Three seconds…

The breath that it took for me to say the words.

Words I thought I would never utter again.

Words that mean so much more to me now than the first time I said them.

Brad is everything that I didn't want and all that I need. I push, and he pulls. He is my yellow. I don't just love Bradley Pierce. He's ingrained in the deepest parts of me. He's under my skin, and I don't mind him living there with me.

To Be Continued...

Don't stop now. Things are just getting started.
Continue Brad & Samantha's enticing journey in A Callous Kind!

Acknowledgments

First and foremost, I want to thank God and my family for continuing to encourage me every day and in everything that I do.

To Nicole Mcclanahan PA & Sarah Cunningham PA, for jumping on board with me and taking care of everything that I couldn't. They are truly amazing.

To Tracie Douglas at Dark Water Covers for the fabulous cover. It's a pleasure to work with you.

To Amber Garcia at Lady Ambers Reviews and PR for her help in promoting this release.

My Facebook Angels, friends, followers, and readers; thank you all for your feedback, laughs, encouragement, and support.

To the wonderful bloggers and authors, thank you for including me in your busy schedules. Your time, posts, reviews, and comments mean so much.

To the entire book community, thank you for accepting me into the fold. It takes courage, time, patience, and a lot of hard work to do what we do. Let's continue to support each other and bring joy to the lives of many through our words.

Author's Note

Everything that anyone does, big or small, plays a huge part in an author's success. I appreciate you all so very much. Thanks for coming along with me on my journey. If you enjoyed reading my book, please consider posting a review on your preferred site, and don't forget to tell your friends about me.

Until Next Time...

About the Author

Angela K. Parker is a country girl with a big heart. She's a South Carolina native with a passion for writing, reading, music, & math. When she's not engaged in any of the above, she's spending time with her family or catching up on the latest movies. She's always had a very active imagination. Now she's putting it to good use.

Connect with the Author

Website: https://angelakparker.com/romance-novels-angela-k-parker/

Email: angelaparkerauthor@gmail.com